DA VINCI RISING

Imagine what would happen if Leonardo da Vinci—the Albert Einstein of the Renaissance—was actually able to build and fly his fabulous flying machine. In this marvelous story of high political intrigue, danger, adventure, and ethical dilemma, Leonardo faces the difficult and dangerous consequences of what happens when you try to turn dreams into reality.

Da Vinci Rising is an alternate history of the highest order, a remarkable recreation of fifteenth-century Florence, where da Vinci, Niccolò Machiavelli, Sandro Botticelli, and Lorenzo the Magnificent are on the verge of disturbing and changing the course of history as we know it.

Winner of the 1996 Nebula Award!

Borgo Press Books by JACK DANN

Da Vinci Rising
The Diamond Pit
The Economy of Light
Jubilee

DA VINCI RISING

JACK DANN

THE BORGO PRESS

MMX

DA VINCI RISING

FIRST EDITION

Published by Wildside Press LLC

www.wildsidebooks.com

DEDICATION

Both of these books are for my lovely pal,

Caren Bohrman

CONTENTS

Chapter One 9

Chapter Two 17

Chapter Three 43

Chapter Four 57

Chapter Five 67

Chapter Six 73

Chapter Seven 89

Chapter Eight 97

About the Author 117

CHAPTER ONE

Dressed as if he were on fire—in a doublet of heliotrope and crimson over a blood-red shirt—Leonardo da Vinci entered the workshop of his master, Andrea Verrochio.

Verrochio had invited a robust and august company of men to what had become one of the most important salons in Florence. The many conversations were loud and the floor was stained with wine. Leonardo's fellow apprentices stood near the walls, discreetly listening and interjecting a word here and there. Normally, Master Andrea cajoled the apprentices to work—he had long given up on Leonardo, the best of them all, who worked when he would—but tonight he had closed the shop. The aged Paolo del Pozzo Toscanelli, who had taught Leonardo mathematics and geography, sat near a huge earthenware jar and a model of the lavabado that would be installed in the old Sacristy of San Lorenzo. A boy with dark intense eyes and a tight accusing mouth stood behind him like a shadow. Leonardo had never seen this boy before; perhaps Toscanelli had but recently taken this waif into his home.

"I want you to meet a young man with whom you

have much in common," Toscanelli said. "His father is also a notary, like yours. He has put young Niccolò in my care. Niccolò is a child of love, also like you, and extremely talented as a poet and playwright and rhetorician. He is interested in everything, and he seems unable to finish anything! But unlike you, Leonardo, he talks very little, isn't that right, Niccolò."

"I am perfectly capable of talking, Ser Toscanelli," the boy said.

"What's your name?" Leonardo asked.

"Ach, forgive me my lack of manners," Toscanelli said. "Master Leonardo, this is Niccolò Machiavelli, son of Bernardo di Niccolò and Bartolomea Nelli. You may have heard of Bartolomea, a religious poetess of great talent."

Leonardo bowed and said with a touch of sarcasm, "I am honored to meet you, young sir."

"I would like you to help this young man with his education," Toscanelli said.

"But I—"

"You are too much of a lone wolf, Leonardo. You must learn to give generously of your talents. Teach him to see as you do, to play the lyre, to paint. Teach him magic and perspective, teach him about the streets, and women, and the nature of light. Show him your flying machine and your sketches of birds. And I guarantee, he will repay you."

"But he's only a boy!"

Niccolò Machiavelli stood before Leonardo, staring at him expectantly, as if concerned. He was a handsome boy, tall and gangly, but his face was unnaturally severe for one so young. Yet he seemed comfortable alone here in this strange place. Merely curious, Leonardo thought.

"What are you called?" Leonardo asked, taking interest.

"Niccolò," the boy said.

"And you have no nickname?"

"I am called Niccolò Machiavelli, that is my name."

"Well, I shall call you Nicco, young sir. Do you have any objections."

After a pause, he said, "No, Maestro," but the glimmer of a smile compressed his thin lips.

"So your new name pleases you somewhat," Leonardo said.

"I find it amusing that you feel it necessary to make my name smaller. Does that make you feel larger?"

Leonardo laughed. "And what is your age?"

"I am almost fifteen."

"But you are really fourteen, is that not so?"

"And you are still but an apprentice to Master Andrea, yet you are truly a master, or so Master Toscanelli has told me. Since you are closer to being a master, wouldn't you prefer men to think of you as such? Or would you rather be treated as an apprentice such as the one there who is in charge of filling glasses with wine? Well, Master Leonardo...?"

Leonardo laughed again, taking a liking to this intelligent boy who acted as if he possessed twice his years, and said, "You may call me Leonardo."

At that moment, Andrea Verrochio walked over to Leonardo with Lorenzo de' Medici in tow. Lorenzo was magnetic, charismatic, and ugly. His face was coarse, overpowered by a large, flattened nose, and he was suffering one of his periodic outbreaks of eczema; his chin and cheeks were covered with a flesh-colored paste. He had a bull-neck and long, straight brown hair, yet he held himself with such grace that he appeared taller than the men around him. His eyes were perhaps his most arresting feature, for they looked at everything with such friendly intensity, as if to see through things and people alike.

"We have in our midst Leonardo da Vinci, the consummate conjurer and prestidigitator," Verrochio said, bowing to Lorenzo de' Medici as he presented Leonardo to him; he spoke loud enough for all to hear. "Leonardo has fashioned a machine that can carry a man in the air like a bird..."

"My sweet friend Andrea has often told me about your inventiveness, Leonardo da Vinci," Lorenzo said, a slight sarcasm in his voice; ironically, he spoke to Leonardo in much the same good-humored yet condescending tone that Leonardo had used when addressing young Machiavelli. "But how do you presume to affect this miracle of flight? Surely not be means of your cranks and pulleys. Will you conjure up the flying beast Geryon, as we read Dante did and so descend upon its neck into the infernal regions? Or will you merely paint yourself into the sky?"

Everyone laughed at that, and Leonardo, who

would not dare to try to seize the stage from Lorenzo, explained, "My most illustrious Lord, you may see that the beating of its wings against the air supports a heavy eagle in the highest and rarest atmosphere, close to the sphere of elemental fire. Again, you may see the air in motion over the sea fill the swelling sails and drive heavily laden ships. Just so could a man with wings large enough and properly connected learn to overcome the resistance of the air and, by conquering it, succeed in subjugating it and rising above it.

"After all," Leonardo continued, "a bird is nothing more than an instrument that works according to mathematical laws, and it is within the capacity of man to reproduce it with all its movements."

"But a man is not a bird," Lorenzo said. "A bird has sinews and muscles that are incomparably more powerful than a man's. If we were constructed so as to have wings, we would have been provided with them by the Almighty."

"Then you think we are too weak to fly?"

"Indeed, I think the evidence would lead reasonable men to that conclusion," Lorenzo said.

"But surely," Leonardo said, "you have seen falcons carrying ducks and eagles carrying hares; and there are times when these birds of prey must double their rate of speed to follow their prey. But they only need a little force to sustain themselves, and to balance themselves on their wings, and flap them in the pathway of the wind and so direct the course of their journeying. A slight movement of the wings is sufficient, and the greater the size of the bird, the slower the movement. It's the same with men, for we possess a greater amount of strength in our legs than our weight requires. In fact, we have twice the amount of strength we need to support ourselves. You can prove this by observing how far the marks of one of your men's feet will sink into the sand of the seashore. If you then order another man to climb upon his back, you can observe how much deeper the foot marks will be. But remove the man from the other's back and order the first man to jump as high as he can, and you will find that the marks of his feet will now make a deeper impression where he has jumped than in the place where he had the other man on his back. That's double proof that a man has more than twice the strength he needs to support himself...more than enough to fly like a bird."

Lorenzo laughed. "Very good, Leonardo. But I would have to see with my own eyes your machine that turns men into birds. Is *that* what you've been spending your precious time doing, instead of working on the statues I commissioned you to repair?"

Leonardo let his gaze drop to the floor.

"Not at all," Verrochio interrupted, "Leonardo has indeed been with me in your gardens applying his talent to the repair of—"

"Show me this machine, painter," Lorenzo said to Leonardo. "I could use such a device to confound my enemies, especially those wearing the colors of the south"—the veiled reference was to Pope Sixtus IV and the Florentine Pazzi family. "Is it ready to be used?"

"Not just yet, Magnificence," Leonardo said. I'm still experimenting."

Everyone laughed, including Lorenzo. "Ah, experimenting is it...well, then I'll pledge you to communicate with me when it's finished. But from your past performance, I think that none of us need worry."

Humiliated, Leonardo could only avert his eyes.

"Tell me, how long do you anticipate that your... experiments will take?"

"I think I could safely estimate that my 'contraption' would be ready for flight in two weeks," Leonardo said, taking the advantage, to everyone's surprise. "I plan to launch my great bird from Swan Mountain in Fiesole."

The studio became a roar of surprised conversation.

Leonardo had no choice except to meet Lorenzo's challenge; if he did not, Lorenzo might ruin his career. As it was, his Magnificence obviously considered Leonardo to be a dilettante, a polymath genius who could not be trusted to bring his commisions to fruition.

"Forgive my caustic remarks, Leonardo, for everyone in this room respects your pretty work," Lorenzo said. "But I will take you up on your promise: in two weeks we travel to Fiesole!"

CHAPTER TWO

One could almost imagine that the great bird was already in flight, hovering in the gauzy morning light like a great, impossible hummingbird. It was a chimerical thing that hung from the high attic ceiling of Leonardo's workshop in Verrocchio's *bottega*: a tapered plank fitted with hand operated cranks, hoops of well-tanned leather, pedals, windlass, oars, and saddle. Great ribbed batlike wings made of cane and fustian and starched taffeta were connected to the broader end of the plank. They were dyed bright red and gold, the colors of the Medici, for it was the Medici who would attend its first flight.

As Leonardo had written in his notebook: *Remember that your bird must imitate only the bat because its webbing forms a framework that gives strength to the wings. If you imitate the birds' wings, you will discover the feathers to be disunited and permeable to the air. But the bat is aided by the membrane which binds the whole and is not pervious.* This was written backwards from right to left in Leonardo's idiosyncratic 'mirror' script that was all but impossible to decipher. Leonardo lived in paranoid fear that his best ideas and inventions would be stolen.

Although he sat before a canvas he was painting, his eyes smarting from the miasmas of varnish and linseed oil and first grade turpentine, Leonardo nervously gazed up at his invention. It filled the upper area of the large room, for its wingspan was over fifteen ells— more than twenty-five feet.

For the past few days Leonardo had been certain that something was not quite right with his great bird, yet he could not divine what it might be. Nor could he sleep well, for he had been having nightmares; no doubt they were a consequence of his apprehensions over his flying machine, which was due to be flown from the top of a mountain in just ten days. His dream was always the same: he would be falling from a great height...without wings, without harness...into a barely luminescent void, while above him the familiar sunlit hills and mountains that overlooked Vinci would be turning vertiginously. And he would awaken in a cold sweat, tearing at his covers, his heart beating in his throat as if to choke him.

Leonardo was afraid of heights. While exploring the craggy and dangerous slopes of Monte Albano as a child, he had fallen from an overhang and almost broken his back. But Leonardo was determined to conquer this and every other fear. He would become as familiar with the airy realms as the birds that soared and rested on the winds. He would make the very air his ally, his support and security.

There was a characteristic knock on the door: two

light taps followed by a loud thump.

"Enter, Andrea, lest the dead wake," Leonardo said without getting up.

Verrocchio stormed in with his foreman Francesco di Simone, a burly, full-faced, middle-aged man whose muscular body was just beginning to go to seed. Francesco carried a silver tray, upon which were placed cold meats, fruit, and two cruses of milk; he laid it on the table beside Leonardo. Both Verrocchio and Francesco had been at work for hours, as was attested by the lime and marble dust that streaked their faces and shook from their clothes. They were unshaven and wore work gowns, although Verrocchio's was more a frock, as if, indeed, he envisioned himself as a priest to art—the unblest 'tenth muse.'

Most likely they had been in one of the outer workshops, for Andrea was having trouble with a terra cotta *risurrezione* relief destined for Lorenzo's villa in Careggi. But this bottega was so busy that Andrea's attention was constantly in demand. "Well, at least *you're* awake," Andrea said to Leonardo as he looked appreciatively at the painting-in-progress. Then he clapped his hands, making such a loud noise that Niccolò, who was fast asleep on his pallet beside Leonardo's, awakened with a cry, as if from a particularly nasty nightmare. Andrea chuckled and said, "Well, good morning, young ser. Perhaps I could have one of the other apprentices find enough work for you to keep you busy during the spine of the morning."

"I apologize, Maestro Andrea, but Maestro Leonardo

and I worked late into the night." Niccolò removed his red, woolen sleeping cap and hurriedly put on a gown that lay on the floor beside his pallet, for like most Florentines, he slept naked.

"Ah, so now it's Maestro Leonardo, is it?" Andrea said good-naturedly. "Well, eat your breakfast, both of you. Today I'm a happy man; I have news."

Niccolò did as he was told, and, in fact, ate like a trencherman, spilling milk on his lap.

"One would never guess that he came from a good family," Andrea said, watching Niccolò stuff his mouth.

"Now tell me your news," Leonardo said.

"It's not all that much to tell." Nevertheless Andrea could not repress a grin. "*Il Magnifico* has informed me that my 'David' will stand prominently in the Palazzo Vecchio over the great staircase."

Leonardo nodded. "But, certainly, you knew Lorenzo would find a place of special honor for such a work of genius."

"I don't know if you compliment me or yourself, Leonardo," Andrea said. "After all, you are the model."

"You took great liberties," Leonardo said. "You may have begun with my features, but you have created something sublime out of the ordinary. You deserve the compliment."

"I fear this pleasing talk will cost me either money or time," Andrea said.

Leonardo laughed. "Indeed, today I must be out of the city."

Andrea gazed up at Leonardo's flying machine and said, "No one would blame you if you backed out of this project, or, at least, allowed someone else to fly your contraption. You need not prove yourself to Lorenzo."

"I would volunteer to fly your mechanical bird, Leonardo," Niccolò said earnestly.

"No, it must be me."

"Was it not to gain experience that Master Toscanelli sent me to you?"

"To gain experience, yes; but not to jeopardize your life," Leonardo said.

"You are not satisfied it will work?" Andrea asked.

"Of course I am, Andrea. If I were not, I would bow before Lorenzo and give him the satisfaction of publicly putting me to the blush."

"Leonardo, be truthful with me," Verrocchio said. "It is to Andrea you speak, not a rich patron."

"Yes, my friend, I am worried," Leonardo confessed. "Something is indeed wrong with my Great Bird, yet I cannot quite put my finger on it. It is most frustrating."

"Then you must not fly it!"

"It will fly, Andrea. I promise you that."

"You have my blessing to take the day off," Verrocchio said.

"I am most grateful," Leonardo said; and they both laughed, knowing that Leonardo would have left for the country with or without Andrea's permission.

"Well, we must be off," Leonardo said to Andrea, who nodded and took his leave.

"Come on, Nicco," Leonardo said, suddenly full of

energy. "Get yourself dressed;" and as Niccolò did so, Leonardo put a few finishing touches on his painting, then quickly cleaned his brushes, hooked his sketch-book onto his belt, and once again craned his neck to stare at his invention that hung from the ceiling. He needed an answer, yet he had not yet formulated the question.

When they were out the door, Leonardo felt that he had forgotten something. "Nicco, fetch me the book Maestro Toscanelli loaned to me...the one he purchased from the Chinese trader. I might wish to read in the country."

"The country?" Niccolò asked, carefully putting the book into a sack, which he carried under his arm.

"Do you object to nature?" Leonardo asked sarcastically. "*Usus est optimum magister*...and in that I agree wholeheartedly with the ancients. Nature herself is the mother of all experience; and experience must be your teacher, for I have discovered that even Aristotle can be mistaken on certain subjects." As they left the bottega, he continued: "But those of Maestro Ficino's Academy, they go about all puffed and pompous, mouthing the eternal aphorisms of Plato and Aristotle like parrots. They might think that because I have not had a literary education, I am uncultured; but they are the fools. They despise me because I am an inventor, but how much more are they to blame for *not* being inventors, these trumpeters and reciters of the works of others. They considered my glass to study the skies and make the moon large a conjuring trick, and do you know why?" Before Niccolò could respond, Leonardo said, "Because they consider sight to be the most untrustworthy of senses, when, in fact, it is the supreme organ. Yet that does not prevent them from wearing spectacles in secret. Hypocrites!"

"You seem very angry, Maestro," Niccolò said to Leonardo.

Embarrassed at having launched into this diatribe, Leonardo laughed at himself and said, "Perhaps I am, but do not worry about it, my young friend."

"Maestro Toscanelli seems to respect the learned men of the Academy," Niccolò said.

"He respects Plato and Aristotle, as well he should. But he does not teach at the Academy, does he? No, instead, he lectures at the school at Santo Spirito for the Augustinian brothers. That should tell you something."

"I think it tells me that you have an ax to grind, Master...and that's also what Maestro Toscanelli told me."

"What else did he tell you, Nicco?" Leonardo asked.

"That I should learn from your strengths and weaknesses, and that you are smarter than everyone in the Academy."

Leonardo laughed at that and said, "You lie very convincingly."

"That, Maestro, comes naturally."

* * * * * * *

The streets were busy and noisy and the sky, which

seemed pierced by the tiled mass of the Duomo and the Palace of the Signoria, was cloudless and sapphire-blue. There was the sweet smell of sausage in the air, and young merchants—practically children—stood behind stalls and shouted at every passerby. This market was called *Il Baccano*, the place of uproar. Leonardo bought some cooked meat, beans, fruit, and a bottle of cheap local wine for Niccolò and himself. They continued on into different neighborhoods and markets. They passed Spanish Moors with their slave retinues from the Ivory Coast; Mamluks in swathed robes and flat turbans; Muscovy Tartars and Mongols from Cathay; and merchants from England and Flanders, who had sold their woolen cloth and were on their way to the Ponte Vecchio to purchase trinkets and baubles. Niccolò was all eye and motion as they passed elegant and beautiful 'butterflies of the night' standing beside their merchant masters under the shade of guild awnings; these whores and mistresses modeled jeweled garlands, and expensive garments of violet, crimson, and peach. Leonardo and Niccolò passed stall after stall—brushing off young hawkers and old, disease-ravaged beggars—and flowed with the crowds of peddlers, citizens, and visitors as if they were flotsam in the sea. Young men of means, dressed in short doublets, wiggled and swayed like young girls through the streets; they roistered and swashbuckled, laughed and sang and bullied, these favored ones. Niccolò could not help but laugh at the scholars and student wanderers from England and Scotland and

Bohemia, for although their *lingua franca* was Latin, their accents were extravagant and overwrought.

"Ho, Leonardo," cried one vendor, then another, as Leonardo and Niccolò turned a corner. Then the screes and cries of birds sounded, for the bird-sellers were shaking the small wooden cages packed with wood pigeons, owls, mousebirds, bee-eaters, humming-birds, crows, blue rockthrushes, warblers, flycatchers, wagtails, hawks, falcons, eagles, and all manner of swans, ducks, chickens, and geese. As Leonardo approached, the birds were making more commotion than the vendors and buyers on the street. "Come here, Master," shouted a red-haired man wearing a stained brown doublet with torn sleeves. His right eye appeared infected, for it was bloodshot, crusted, and tearing. He shook two cages, each containing hawks; one bird was brown with a forked chestnut tail, and the other was smaller and black with a notched tail. They banged against the wooden bars and snapped danger-ously. "Buy these, Maestro Artista, please...they are just what you need, are they not? And look how many doves I have, do they not interest you, good Master?"

"Indeed, the hawks are fine specimens," Leonardo said, drawing closer, while the other vendors called and shouted to him, as if he were carrying the grail itself. "How much?"

"Ten denari."

"Three."

"Eight."

"Four, and if that is not satisfactory, I can easily talk

to your neighbor, who is flapping his arms as if he, himself, could fly."

"Agreed," said the vendor, resigned.

"And the doves?"

"For how many, Maestro?"

"For the lot."

While Leonardo dickered with the bird vendor, Niccolò wandered about. He looked at the multicolored birds and listened, as he often did. With ear and eye he would learn the ways of the world. Leonardo, it appeared, was known in this market; and a small crowd of hecklers and the merely curious began to form around him. The hucksters made much of it, trying to sell to whomever they could.

"He's as mad as Ajax," said an old man who had just sold a few chickens and doves and was as animated as the street thugs and young beggars standing around him. "He'll let them all go, watch, you'll see."

"I've heard tell he won't eat meat," said one matronly woman to another. "He lets the birds go free because he feels sorry for the poor creatures."

"Well, to be safe, don't look straight at him," said the other woman as she made the sign of the cross. He might be a sorcerer. He could put evil in your eye, and enter right into your soul!"

Her companion shivered and followed suit by crossing herself.

"Nicco," Leonardo shouted, making himself heard above the din. "Come here and help me." When Niccolò appeared, Leonardo said, "If you could raise your thoughts from those of butterflies"—and by that he meant whores—"you might learn something of observation and the ways of science." He thrust his hand into the cage filled with doves and grasped one. The tiny bird made a frightened noise; as Leonardo took it from its cage, he could feel its heart beating in his palm. Then he opened his hand and watched the dove fly away. The crowd laughed and jeered and applauded and shouted for more. He took another bird out of its cage and released it. His eyes squinted almost shut; and as he gazed at the dove beating its wings so hard that, but for the crowd, one could have heard them clap, he seemed lost in thought. "Now, Nicco, I want you to let the birds free, one by one."

"Why me?" Niccolò asked, somehow loath to seize the birds.

"Because I wish to draw," Leonardo said. "Is this chore too difficult for you?"

"I beg your pardon, Maestro," Niccolò said, as he reached into the cage. He had a difficult time catching a bird. Leonardo seemed impatient and completely oblivious to the shouts and taunts of the crowd around him. Niccolò let go of one bird, and then another, while Leonardo sketched. Leonardo stood very still, entranced; only his hand moved like a ferret over the bleached folio, as if it had a life and will of its own.

As Niccolò let fly another bird, Leonardo said, "Do you see, Nicco, the bird in its haste to climb strikes its outstretched wings together above its body. "Now look how it uses its wings and tail in the same way that a swimmer uses his arms and legs in the water; it's the very same principle. It seeks the air currents, which, invisible, roil around the buildings of our city. And there, its speed is checked by the opening and spreading out of the tail... Let fly another one. Can you see how the wing separates to let the air pass?" and he wrote a note in his mirror script below one of his sketches: *Make device so that when the wing rises up it remains pierced through, and when it falls it is all united.* "Another," he called to Niccolò. And after the bird disappeared, he made another note: *The speed is checked by the opening and spreading out of the tail. Also, the opening and lowering of the tail, and the simultaneous spreading of the wings to their full extent, arrests their swift movement.*

"That's the end of it," Niccolò said, indicating the empty cages. "Do you wish to free the hawks?"

"No," Leonardo said, distracted. "We will take them with us," and Leonardo and Niccolò made their way through the crowd, which now began to disperse. As if a reflection of Leonardo's change of mood, clouds darkened the sky; and the bleak, refuse-strewn streets took on a more dangerous aspect. The other bird vendors called to Leonardo, but he ignored them, as he did Niccolò. He stared intently into his notebook as he walked, as if he were trying to decipher ancient runes.

They passed the wheel of the bankrupts. Defeated men sat around a marble inlay that was worked into the piazza in the design of a cartwheel. A crowd had formed, momentarily, to watch a debtor, who had been stripped naked, being pulled to the roof of the market by a rope. Then there was a great shout as he was dropped headfirst onto the smooth, cold, marble floor.

A sign attached to one of the market posts read:

> Give good heed to the small sums thou spendest out of the house, for it is they which empty the purse and consume wealth; and they go on continually. And do not buy all the good victuals which thou seest, for the house is like a wolf: the more thou givest it, the more doth it devour.

The man dropped by the rope was dead.

Leonardo put his arm around Niccolò's shoulders, as if to shield him from death. But he was suddenly afraid...afraid that his own 'inevitable hour' might not be far away; and he remembered his recurring dream of falling into the abyss. He shivered, his breath came quick, and his skin felt clammy, as if he had just been jolted awake. Just now, on some deep level, he believed that the poisonous phantasms of dreams were real. If they took hold of the soul of the dreamer, they could effect his entire world.

Leonardo saw his Great Bird falling and breaking apart. And he was falling through cold depths that were as deep as the reflections of lanterns in dark water.

"Leonardo? *Leonardo!*"

"Do not worry. I am fine, my young friend," Leonardo said.

They talked very little until they were in the country,

in the high, hilly land north of Florence. Here were meadows and grassy fields, valleys and secret grottos, small roads traversed by ox carts and pack trains, vineyards and cane thickets, dark copses of pine and chestnut and cypress, and olive trees that shimmered like silver hangings each time the wind breathed past their leaves. The deep red tiles of farmstead roofs and the brownish-pink colonnaded villas seemed to be part of the line and tone of the natural countryside. The clouds that had darkened the streets of Florence had disappeared; and the sun was high, bathing the countryside in that golden light particular to Tuscany, a light that purified and clarified as if it were itself the manifestation of desire and spirit.

And before them, in the distance, was Swan Mountain. It rose 1,300 feet to its crest, and looked to be pale gray-blue in the distance.

Leonardo and Niccolò stopped in a meadow perfumed with flowers and gazed at the mountain. Leonardo felt his worries weaken, as they always did when he was in the country. He took a deep breath of the heady air and felt his soul awaken and quicken to the world of nature and the *oculus spiritalis*: the world of angels.

"That would be a good mountain from which to test your Great Bird," Niccolò said.

"I thought that, too, for it's very close to Florence. But I've since changed my mind. Vinci is not so far away; and there are good mountains there, too." Then after a pause, Leonardo said, "And I do not wish to die here. If death should be my fate, I wish it to be in familiar surroundings."

Niccolò nodded, and he looked as severe and serious as he had when Leonardo had first met him, like an old man inhabiting a boy's body.

"Come now, Nicco," Leonardo said, resting the cage on the ground and sitting down beside it, "let's enjoy this time, for who knows what awaits us later. Let's eat." With that, Leonardo spread out a cloth and set the food upon it as if it were a table. The hawks flapped their wings and slammed against the wooden bars of the cages. Leonardo tossed them each a small piece of sausage.

"I heard gossip in the piazza of the bird vendors that you refuse to eat meat," Niccolò said.

"Ah, did you, now. And what do you think of that?"

Niccolò shrugged. "Well, I have never seen you eat meat."

Leonardo ate a piece of bread and sausage, which he washed down with wine. "Now you have."

"But then why would people say that—"

"Because I don't usually eat meat. They're correct, for I believe that eating too much meat causes to collect what Aristotle defined as cold black bile. That, in turn, afflicts the soul with melancholia. Maestro Toscanelli's friend Ficino believes the same, but for all the wrong reasons. For him magic and astrology take precedence over reason and experience. But be that as it may, I must be very careful that people do not think of me as a follower of the Cathars, lest I be branded a heretic."

"I have not heard of them."

"They follow the teaching of the pope Bogomil, who believed that our entire visible world was created by the Adversary rather than by God. Thus to avoid imbibing the essence of Satan, they forfeit meat. Yet they eat vegetables and fish." Leonardo laughed and pulled a face to indicate they were crazy. "They could at least be consistent."

Leonardo ate quickly, which was his habit, for he could never seem to enjoy savoring food as others did. He felt that eating, like sleeping, was simply a necessity that took him away from whatever interested him at the moment.

And there was a whole world pulsing in the sunlight around him; like a child, he wanted to investigate its secrets.

"Now...watch," he said to Niccolò, who was still eating; and he let loose one of the hawks. As it flew away, Leonardo made notes, scribbling with his left hand, and said, "You see, Nicco, it searches now for a current of the wind." He loosed the other one. "These birds beat their wings only until they reach the wind, which must be blowing at a great elevation, for look how high they soar. Then they are almost motionless."

Leonardo watched the birds circle overhead, then glide toward the mountains. He felt transported, as if he too were gliding in the Empyrean heights. "They're hardly moving their wings now. They repose in the air as we do on a pallet."

"Perhaps you should follow their example."

"What do you mean?" Leonardo asked.

"Fix your wings on the Great Bird. Instead of beating the air, they would remain stationary."

"And by what mode would the machine be propelled?" Leonardo asked; but he answered his own question, for immediately the idea of the Archimedian Screw came to mind. He remembered seeing children playing with toy whirlybirds: by pulling a string, a propeller would be made to rise freely into the air. His hand sketched, as if thinking on its own. He drew a series of sketches of leaves gliding back and forth, falling to the ground. He drew various screws and propellers. There might be something useful...

"Perhaps if you could just catch the current, then you would not have need of human power," Niccolò said. "You could fix your bird to soar...somehow."

Leonardo patted Niccolò on the shoulder, for, indeed, the child was bright. But it was all wrong; it *felt* wrong. "No, my young friend," he said doggedly, as if he had come upon a wall that blocked his thought, "the wings must be able to row through the air like a bird's. That is nature's method, the most efficient way."

Restlessly, Leonardo wandered the hills. Niccolò finally complained of being tired and stayed behind, comfortably situated in a shady copse of mossy-smelling cypresses.

Leonardo walked on alone.

Everything was perfect: the air, the warmth, the smells and sounds of the country. He could almost apprehend the pure forms of everything around him, the phantasms reflected in the *proton organon*: the mirrors of his soul. But not quite...

Indeed, something was wrong, for instead of the bliss, which Leonardo had so often experienced in the country, he felt thwarted...lost.

Thinking of the falling leaf, which he had sketched in his notebook, he wrote: *If a man has a tent roof of caulked linen twelve ells broad and twelve ells high, he will be able to let himself fall from any great height without danger to himself.*" He imagined a pyramidal parachute, yet considered it too large and bulky and heavy to carry on the Great Bird. He wrote another hasty note: *Use leather bags, so a man falling from a height of six brachia will not injure himself, falling either into water or upon land.*

He continued walking, aimlessly. He sketched constantly, as if without conscious thought: grotesque figures and caricatured faces, animals, impossible mechanisms, studies of various madonnas with children, imaginary landscapes, and all manner of actual flora and fauna. He drew a three-dimensional diagram of a toothed gearing and pulley system and an apparatus for making lead. He made a note to locate Albertus Magnus' *On Heaven and Earth*—perhaps Toscanelli had a copy. His thoughts seemed to flow like the Arno, from one subject to another, and yet he could not position himself in that psychic place of languor and bliss, which he imagined to be the perfect realm of Platonic forms.

As birds flew overhead, he studied them and sketched

feverishly. Leonardo had an extraordinarily quick eye, and he could discern movements that others could not see. He wrote in tiny letters beside his sketches: *Just as we may see a small imperceptible movement of the rudder turn a ship of marvelous size loaded with very heavy cargo—and also amid such weight of water pressing upon its every beam and in the teeth of impetuous winds that envelop its mighty sails—so, too, do birds support themselves above the course of the winds without beating their wings. Just a slight movement of wing or tail, serving them to enter either below or above the wind, suffices to prevent their fall.* Then he added, *When, without the assistance of the wind and without beating its wings, the bird remains in the air in the position of equilibrium, this shows that the center of gravity is coincident with the center of resistance.*

"Ho, Leonardo," shouted Niccolò, who was running after him. The boy was out of breath; he carried the brown sack, which contained some leftover food, most likely, and Maestro Toscanelli's book. "You've been gone over three hours!"

"And is that such a long time?" Leonardo asked.

"It is for me. What are you doing?"

"Just walking...and thinking." After a beat, Leonardo said, "But you have a book, why didn't you read it?"

Niccolò smiled and said, " I tried, but then I fell asleep."

"So now we have the truth," Leonardo said. "Nicco, why don't you return to the bottega? I must remain here...to think. And you are obviously bored."

"That's all right, Maestro," Niccolò said anxiously. "If I can stay with you, I won't be bored. I promise."

Leonardo smiled, in spite of himself, and said, "Tell me what you've gleaned from the little yellow book."

"I can't make it out...yet. It seems to be all about light."

"So Maestro Toscanelli told me. Its writings are very old and concern memory and the circulation of light." Leonardo could not resist teasing his apprentice. "Do you find your memory much improved after reading it?"

Niccolò shrugged, as if it was of no interest to him, and Leonardo settled down in a grove of olive trees to read *The Secret of the Golden Flower*; it took him less than an hour, for the book was short. Niccolò ate some fruit and then fell asleep again, seemingly without any trouble.

Most of the text seemed to be magical gibberish, yet suddenly these words seemed to open him up:

> There are a thousand spaces, and the light-flower of heaven and earth fills them all. Just so does the light-flower of the individual pass through heaven and cover the earth. And when the light begins to circulate, all of heaven and the earth, all the mountains and rivers—every-thing—begins to circulate with light. The key is to concentrate your own seed-flower in the eyes. But be careful, children, for if one day you do not practice meditation, this light will stream out, to be lost who knows where...?

Perhaps he fell asleep, for he imagined himself staring at the walls of his great and perfect mnemonic construct: the memory cathedral. It was pure white and smooth as dressed stone...it was a church for all his experience and knowledge, whether holy or profane. Maestro Toscanelli had taught him long ago how to construct a church in his imagination, a storage place of images—hundreds of thousands of them—which would represent everything Leonardo wished to remember. Leonardo caught all the evanescent and ephemeral stuff of time and trapped it in this place... all the happenings of his life, everything he had seen and read and heard; all the pain and frustration and love and joy were neatly shelved and ordered inside the colonnaded courts, chapels, vestries, porches, towers, and crossings of his memory cathedral.

He longed to be inside, to return to sweet, comforting memory; he would dismiss the ghosts of fear that haunted its dark catacombs. But now he was seeing the cathedral from a distant height, from the summit of Swan Mountain, and it was as if his cathedral had somehow become a small part of what his memory held and his eyes saw. It was as if his soul could expand to fill Heaven and earth, the past and the future. Leonardo experienced a sudden, vertiginous sensation of freedom; indeed, heaven and earth seemed to be filled with a thousand spaces. It was just as he had read in the ancient book: everything was circulating with pure light...blinding, cleansing light that coruscated down the hills and mountains like rainwater, that floated in the air like mist, that heated the grass and meadows to radiance.

He felt bliss.

Everything was preternaturally clear; it was as if he was seeing into the essence of things.

And then with a shock he felt himself slipping, falling from the mountain.

This was his recurring dream, his nightmare: to fall...without wings, without harness...into the void. Yet every detail registered: the face of the mountain, the mossy crevasses, the smells of wood and stone and decomposition, the screeing of a hawk, the glint of a stream below, the roofs of farmhouses, the geometrical demarcations of fields, and the spiraling wisps of cloud that seemed to be woven into the sky. But then he tumbled and descended into palpable darkness, into a frightful abyss that showed no feature and no bottom.

Leonardo screamed to awaken back into daylight, for he knew this blind place, which the immortal Dante had explored and described. But now he felt the horrid bulk of the flying monster Geryon beneath him, supporting him...this, the same beast that had carried Dante into *Malebolge*: the Eighth Circle of Hell. The monster was slippery with filth and smelled of death and putrefaction; the air itself was foul, and Leonardo could hear behind him the thrashing of the creature's scorpion tail. Yet it also seemed that he could hear Dante's divine voice whispering to him, drawing him through the very walls of Hades into blinding light.

But now he was held aloft by the Great Bird, his

own invention. He soared over the trees and hills and meadows of Fiesole, and then south, to fly over the roofs and balconies and spires of Florence herself.

Leonardo flew without fear, as if the wings were his own flesh. He moved his arms easily, working the great wings that beat against the calm, spring air that was as warm as his own breath. But rather than resting upon his apparatus, he now hung below it. He operated a windlass with his hands to raise one set of wings and kicked a pedal with his heels to lower the other set of wings. Around his neck was a collar, which controlled a rudder that was effectively the tail of this bird.

This was certainly not the machine that hung in Verrocchio's bottega. Yet with its double set of wings, it seemed more like a great insect than a bird, and—

Leonardo awakened with a jolt, to find himself staring at a horsefly feeding upon his hand.

Could he have been sleeping with his eyes open, or had this been a waking dream? He shivered, for his sweat was cold on his arms and chest.

He shouted, awakening Niccolò, and immediately began sketching and writing in his notebook. "I have it!" he said to Niccolò. "Double wings like a fly will provide the power I need. You see, it is just as I told you: nature provides. Art and invention are merely imitation." He drew a man hanging beneath an apparatus with hand-operated cranks and pedals to work the wings. Then he studied the fly, which still buzzed around him, and wrote: *The lower wings are more slanting than those above, both as to length and as to breadth. The fly when it hovers in the air upon its wings beats its wings with great speed and din, raising them from the horizontal position up as high as the wing is long. And as it raises them, it brings them forward in a slanting position in such a way as almost to strike the air edgewise.* Then he drew a design for the rudder assembly. "How could I not have seen that just as a ship needs a rudder, so, too, would my machine?" he said. "It will act as the tail of a bird. And by hanging the operator below the wings, equilibrium will be more easily maintained. There," he said, standing up and pulling Niccolò to his feet. "Perfection!"

He sang one of Lorenzo de Medici's bawdy inventions and danced around Niccolò, who seemed confused by his master's strange behavior. He grabbed the boy's arms and swung him around in a circle.

"Perhaps the women watching you free the birds were right," Niccolò said. "Perhaps you *are* as mad as Ajax."

"Perhaps I am," Leonardo said, "but I have a lot of work to do, for the Great Bird must be changed if it is to fly for *Il Magnifico* next week." He placed the book of the Golden Flower in the sack, handed it to Niccolò, and began walking in the direction of the city.

It was already late afternoon.

"I'll help you with your machine," Niccolò said.

"Thank you, I'll need you for many errands."

That seemed to satisfy the boy. "Why did you shout and then dance as you did, Maestro?" Niccolò asked, concerned. He followed a step behind Leonardo, who seemed to be in a hurry.

Leonardo laughed and slowed his stride until Niccolò was beside him. "It's difficult to explain. Suffice it to say that solving the riddle of my Great Bird made me happy."

"But how did you do it? I thought you had fallen asleep."

"I had a dream," Leonardo said. "It was a gift from the poet Dante Alighieri."

"*He* gave you the answer?" Niccolò asked, incredulous.

"That he did, Nicco."

"Then you *do* believe in spirits."

"No, Nicco, just in dreams."

CHAPTER THREE

In the streets and markets, people gossiped of a certain hermit—a champion—who had come from Volterra, where he had been ministering to the lepers in a hospital. He had come here to preach and harangue and save the city. He was a young man, and some had claimed to have seen him walking barefoot past the Church of Salvatore. They said he was dressed in the poorest of clothes with only a wallet on his back. His face was bearded and sweet, and his eyes were blue; certainly he was a manifestation of the Christ himself, stepping on the very paving stones that modern Florentines walked. He had declared that the days to follow would bring harrowings, replete with holy signs, for so he had been told by both the Angel Raphael and Saint John, who had appeared to him in their flesh, as men do to other men, and not in a dream.

It was said that he preached to the Jews in their poor quarter and also to the whores and beggars; and he was also seen standing upon the *ringheiera* of the *Signore* demanding an audience with the 'Eight'. But they sent him away. So now there could be no intercession for what was about to break upon Florence.

The next day, a Thursday, one of the small bells of Santa Maria de Fiore broke loose and fell, breaking the skull of a stonemason passing below. By a miracle, he lived, although a bone had to be removed from his skull.

But it was seen as a sign, nevertheless.

And on Friday, a boy of twelve fell from the large bell of the Palagio and landed on the gallery. He died several hours later.

By week's end, four families in the city and eight in the *Borgo di Ricorboli* were stricken with fever and *buboes*, the characteristic swellings of what had come to be called "the honest plague." There were more reports of fever and death every day thereafter, for the Black Reaper was back upon the streets, wending his way through homes and hospitals, cathedrals and taverns, and whorehouses and nunneries alike. It was said that he had a companion, the hag Lachesis, who followed after him while she wove an ever-lengthening tapestry of death; hers was an accounting of 'the debt we must all pay', created from her never-ending skein of black thread.

One hundred and twenty people had died in the churches and hospitals by *nella quidtadecima*: the full moon. There were twenty-five deaths alone at *Santa Maria Nuova*. The 'Eight' of the Signoria duly issued a notice of health procedures to be followed by all Florentines; the price of foodstuffs rose drastically; and although Lorenzo's police combed the streets for the spectral hermit, he was nowhere to be found within the precincts of the city.

Lorenzo and his retinue fled to his villa at Careggi. But rather than follow suit and leave the city for the safety of the country, Verrocchio elected to remain in his bottega. He gave permission to his apprentices to quit the city until the plague abated, if they had the resources; but most, in fact, stayed with him.

The bottega seemed to be in a fervor.

One would think that the deadline for every commission was tomorrow. Verrocchio's foreman Francesco kept a tight and sure rein on the apprentices, pressing them into a twelve to fourteen hour schedule; and they worked as they had when they constructed the bronze palla that topped the dome of Santa Maria dell Fiore, as if quick hands and minds were the only weapons against the ennui upon which the Black Fever might feed. Francesco had become invaluable to Leonardo, for he was quicker with things mechanical than Verrocchio himself; and Francesco helped him design an ingenious plan by which the flying machine could be collapsed and dismantled and camouflaged for easy transportation to Vinci. The flying machine, at least, was complete; again, thanks to Francesco who made certain that Leonardo had a constant supply of strong-backed apprentices and material.

Leonardo's studio was a mess, a labyrinth of footpaths that wound past bolts of cloth, machinery, stacks of wood and leather, jars of paint, sawhorses, and various gearing devices; the actual flying machine took up the center of the great room. Surrounding it were drawings, insects mounted on boards, a table covered with birds and bats in various stages of vivisection, and constructions of the various parts of the redesigned flying machine—artificial wings, rudders, and flap valves.

The noxious odors of turpentine mixed with the various perfumes of decay; these smells disturbed Leonardo not at all, for they reminded him of his childhood when he kept all manner of dead animals in his room to study and paint. All other work—the paintings and terra-cotta sculptures—were piled in one corner. Leonardo and Niccolò could no longer sleep in the crowded, foul-smelling studio; they had laid their pallets down in the young apprentice Tista's room.

Tista was a tall, gangly boy with a shock of blond hair. Although he was about the same age as Niccolò, it was as if he had become Niccolò's apprentice. The boys had become virtually inseparable. Niccolò seemed to relish teaching Tista about life, art, and politics; but then Niccolò had a sure sense of how people behaved, even if he lacked experience. He was a natural teacher, more so than Leonardo. For Leonardo's part, he didn't mind having the other boy underfoot and had, in fact, become quite fond of him. But Leonardo was preoccupied with his work. The Black Death had given him a reprieve—just enough time to complete and test his machine—for not only did *Il Magnifico* agree to rendezvous in Vinci rather than Pistoia, he himself set the date forward another fortnight.

It was unbearably warm in the studio as Niccolò

helped Leonardo remove the windlass mechanism and twin 'oars' from the machine, which were to be packed into a numbered, wooden container. "It's getting close," Niccolò said, after the parts were fitted securely into the box. "Tista tells me that he heard a family living near the Porta alla Croce caught fever."

"Well, we shall be on our way at dawn," Leonardo said. "You shall have the responsibility of making certain that everything is properly loaded and in its proper place."

Niccolò seemed very pleased with that; he had, in fact, proven himself to be a capable worker and organizer. "But I still believe we should wait until the dark effluviums have evaporated from the air. At least until after the *becchini* have carried the corpses to their graves."

"Then we will leave after first light," Leonardo said.

"Good."

"You might be right about the possible contagion of corpses and *becchini*. But as to your effluviums..."

"Best not to take chances," Verrocchio said; he had been standing in the doorway and peering into the room like a boy who had not yet been caught sneaking through the house. He held the door partially closed so that it framed him, as if he were posing for his own portrait; and the particular glow of the late afternoon sun seemed to transform and subdue his rather heavy features.

"I think it is as the astrologers say: a conjunction of planets," Verrocchio continued. "It was so during the great blight of 1345. But that was a conjunction of *three* planets. Very unusual. It will not be like that now, for the conjunction is not nearly so perfect."

"You'd be better to come to the country with us than listen to astrologers," Leonardo said.

"I cannot leave my family. I've told you."

"Then bring them along. My father is already in Vinci preparing the main house for Lorenzo and his retinue. You could think of it as a business holiday; think of the commissions that might fall your way."

"I think I have enough of those for the present," Andrea said.

"That does not sound like Andrea del Verrocchio," Leonardo said, teasing.

"My sisters and cousins refuse to leave," Andrea said. "And who would feed the cats?" he said, smiling, then sighing. He seemed resigned and almost relieved. "My fate is in the lap of the gods...as it has always been. And so is yours, my young friend."

* * * * * * *

The two-day journey was uneventful, and they soon arrived in Vinci.

The town of Leonardo's youth was a fortified keep dominated by a medieval castle and its campanile, surrounded by fifty brownish-pink brick houses. Their red tiled roofs were covered with a foliage of chestnut and pine and cypress, and vines of grape and cane thickets brought the delights of earth and shade to the very walls and windows. The town with its crumbling walls and single arcaded alley was situated on the elevated spur of a mountain; it overlooked a valley blanketed with olive trees that turned silver when stirred by the wind. Beyond was the valley of Lucca, green and purple-shadowed and ribboned with mountain streams; and Leonardo remembered that when the rain had cleansed the air, the crags and peaks of the Apuan Alps near Massa and Cozzile could be clearly seen.

Now that Leonardo was here, he realized how homesick he had been. The sky was clear and the air pellucid; but the poignancy of his memories clouded his vision, as he imagined himself being swept back to his childhood days, once again riding with his Uncle Francesco, whom they called '*lazzarone*' because he did not choose to restrict his zealous enjoyment of life with a profession. But Leonardo and the much older Francesco had been like two privileged boys—princes, riding from farmstead to mill and all around the valley collecting rents for Leonardo's grandfather, the patriarch of the family: the gentle and punctilious Antonio da Vinci.

Leonardo led his apprentices down a cobbled road and past a rotating dovecote on a long pole to a cluster of houses surrounded by gardens, barns, peasant huts, tilled acreage, and the uniform copses of Mulberry trees, which his Uncle Francesco had planted. Francesco, 'the lazy one,' had been experimenting with sericulture, which could prove to be very lucrative indeed, for the richest and most powerful guild in

Florence was the *Arte della Seta*: the silk weavers.

"Leonardo, ho!" shouted Francesco from the courtyard of the large, neatly kept, main house, which had belonged to Ser Antonio. It was stone and roofed with red tile, and looked like the ancient long-houses of the French; but certainly no animals would be kept in the home of Piero da Vinci: Leonardo's father.

Like his brother, Francesco had dark curly hair that was graying at the temples and thinning at the crown. Francesco embraced Leonardo, nearly knocking the wind out of him, and said, "You have caused substantial havoc in this house, my good nephew! Your father is quite anxious."

"I'm sure of that," Leonardo said as he walked into the hall. "It's wonderful to see you, Uncle."

Beyond this expansive, lofted room were several sleeping chambers, two fireplaces, a kitchen and pantry, and workrooms, which sometimes housed the peasants who worked the various da Vinci farmholds; there was a level above with three more rooms and a fireplace; and ten steps below was the cellar where Leonardo used to hide the dead animals he had found. The house was immaculate: how Leonardo's father must have oppressed the less than tidy Francesco and Alessandra to make it ready for Lorenzo and his guests.

His third wife, Margherita di Guglielmo, was nursing his first legitimate son; no doubt that accorded her privileges.

This room was newly fitted-out with covered beds, chests, benches, and a closet cabinet to accommodate several of the lesser luminaries in *Il Magnifico*'s entourage. Without a doubt, Leonardo's father would give the First Citizen his own bedroom.

Leonardo sighed. He craved his father's love, but their relationship had always been awkward and rather formal, as if Leonardo were his apprentice rather than his son.

Piero came down the stairs from his chamber above to meet Leonardo. He wore his magisterial robes and a brimless, silk *berretta* cap, as if he were expecting Lorenzo and his entourage at any moment. "Greetings, my son."

"Greetings to you, father," Leonardo said, bowing.

Leonardo and his father embraced. Then tightly grasping Leonardo's elbow, Piero asked, "May I take you away from your company for a few moments?"

"Of course, Father," Leonardo said politely, allowing himself to be led upstairs.

They entered a writing room, which contained a long, narrow clerical desk, a master's chair, and a sitting bench decorated with two octagonally-shaped pillows; the floor was tiled like a chessboard. A clerk sat upon a stool behind the desk and made a great show of writing in a large, leather-bound ledger. Austere though the room appeared, it revealed a parvenu's taste for comfort; for Piero was eager to be addressed as *messer*, rather than *ser*, and to carry a sword, which was the prerogative of a knight. "Will you excuse us, Vittore?" Piero said to the clerk. The young man rose, bowed, and left the room.

"Yes, father?" Leonardo asked, expecting the worst.

"I don't know whether to scold you or congratulate you."

"The latter would be preferable."

Piero smiled and said, "Andrea has apprised me that *Il Magnifico* has asked for you to work in his gardens."

"Yes."

"I am very proud."

"Thank you, father."

"So you see, I was correct in keeping you to the grindstone."

Leonardo felt his neck and face grow warm. "You mean by taking everything I earned so I could not save enough to pay for my master's matriculation fee in the Painters' Guild?"

"That money went to support the family...your family."

"And now you—or rather the family—will lose that income."

"My concern is not, nor was it ever, the money," Piero said. "It was properly forming your character, of which I am still in some doubt."

"Thank you."

"I'm sorry, but as your father, it is my duty—" He paused. Then, as if trying to be more conciliatory, he said, "You could hardly do better than to have Lorenzo for a patron. But he would have never noticed you, if I had not made it possible for you to remain with Andrea."

"You left neither Andrea nor I any choice."

"Be that as it may, Master Andrea made certain that you produced and completed the projects he assigned to you. At least he tried to prevent you from running off and cavorting with your limp-wristed, degenerate friends."

"Ah, you mean those who are not in *Il Magnifico*'s retinue."

"Don't you dare to be insolent."

"I apologize, father," Leonardo said, but he had become sullen.

"You're making that face again."

"I'm sorry if I offend you."

"You don't offend me, you—" He paused, then said, "You've put our family in an impossible position."

"What do you mean?"

"Your business here with the Medici."

"It does not please you to host the First Citizen?" Leonardo asked.

"You have made a foolish bet with him, and will certainly become the monkey. Our name—"

"Ah, yes, that is, of course, all that worries you. But I shall not fail, father. You can then take full credit for any honor I might bring to our good name."

"Only birds and insects can fly."

"And those who bear the name da Vinci." But Piero would not be mollified. Leonardo sighed and said, "Father, I shall try not to disappoint you." He bowed respectfully and turned toward the door.

"Leonardo!" his father said, as if he were speaking to a child. "I have not excused you."

"May I be excused, then, father?"

"Yes, you may." But then Piero called him back.

"Yes, father?" Leonardo asked, pausing at the door.

"I forbid you to attempt this...experiment."

"I am sorry, father; but I cannot turn tail now."

"I will explain to *Il Magnifico* that you are my first-born."

"Thank you, but—"

"Your safety is my responsibility," Piero said, and then he said, "I worry for you!" Obviously, these words were difficult for him. If their relationship had been structured differently, Leonardo would have crossed the room to embrace his father; and they would have spoken directly. But as robust and lusty as Piero was, he could not accept any physical display of emotion.

After a pause, Leonardo asked, "Will you do me the honor of watching me fly upon the wind?" He ventured a smile. "It will be a da Vinci, not a Medici or a Pazzi, who will be soaring in the heavens closest to God."

"I suppose I shall have to keep up appearances," Piero said; then he raised an eyebrow, as if questioning his place in the scheme of these events. He looked at his son and smiled sadly.

Though once again Leonardo experienced the unbridgeable distance between himself and his father, the tension between them dissolved.

"You are welcome to remain here," Piero said.

"You will have little enough room when Lorenzo and his congregation arrive," Leonardo said. "And I shall need quiet in which to work and prepare; it's been fixed for us to lodge with Achattabrigha di Piero del Vacca."

"When are you expected?"

"We should leave now. Uncle Francesco said he would accompany us."

Piero nodded. "Please give my warmest regards to your mother."

"I shall be happy to do so."

"Are you at all curious to see your new brother?" Piero asked, as if it were an afterthought.

"Of course I am, father."

Piero took his son's arm, and they walked to Margherita's bedroom.

Leonardo could feel his father trembling.

And for those few seconds, he actually felt that he was his father's son.

CHAPTER FOUR

The Great Bird was perched on the edge of a ridge at the summit of a hill near Vinci that Leonardo had selected. It looked like a gigantic dragonfly, its fabric of fustian and silk sighing, as the expansive double wings shifted slightly in the wind. Niccolò, Tista, and Leonardo's stepfather Achattabrigha kneeled under the wings and held fast to the pilot's harness. Zoroastro da Peretola and Lorenzo de Credi, apprentices of Andrea Verrochio, stood twenty-five feet apart and steadied the wing tips; it almost seemed that their arms were filled with outsized jousting pennons of blue and gold. These two could be taken as caricatures of *Il Magnifico* and his brother Giuliano, for Zoroastro was swarthy, rough-skinned, and ugly-looking beside the sweetly handsome Lorenzo de Credi. Such was the contrast between Lorenzo and Giuliano di Medici, who stood with Leonardo a few feet away from the Great Bird. Giuliano looked radiant in the morning sun while Lorenzo seemed to be glowering, although he was most probably simply concerned for Leonardo.

Zoroastro, ever impatient, looked toward Leonardo and shouted, "We're ready for you, Maestro."

Leonardo nodded, but Lorenzo caught him and said, "Leonardo, there is no need for this. I will love you as I do Giuliano, no matter whether you choose to fly...or let wisdom win out."

Leonardo smiled and said, "I will fly *fide et amore.*"

By faith and love.

"You shall have both," Lorenzo said; and he walked beside Leonardo to the edge of the ridge and waved to the crowd standing far below on the edge of a natural clearing where Leonardo was to land triumphant. But the clearing was surrounded by a forest of pine and cypress, which from his vantage looked like a multitude of rough-hewn lances and halberds. A great shout went up, honoring the First Citizen: the entire village was there—from peasant to squire, invited for the occasion by *Il Magnifico,* who had erected a great, multi-colored tent; his attendants and footmen had been cooking and preparing for a feast since dawn. His sister Bianca, Angelo Poliziano, Pico Della Mirandola, Bartolomeo Scala, and Leonardo's friend Sandro Botticelli were down there, too, hosting the festivities.

They were all on tenterhooks, eager for the Great Bird to fly.

Leonardo waited until Lorenzo had received his due; but then not to be outdone, he, too, bowed and waved his arms theatrically. The crowd below cheered their favorite son, and Leonardo turned away to position himself in the harness of his flying machine. He had seen his mother Caterina, a tiny figure nervously looking upward, whispering devotions, her hand cupped above her eyes to cut the glare of the sun. His father Piero stood beside Giuliano de Medici; both men were dressed as if for a hunt. Piero did not speak to Leonardo. His already formidable face was drawn and tight, just as if he were standing before a magistrate awaiting a decision on a case.

Lying down in a prone position on the fore-shortened plank pallet below the wings and windlass mechanism, Leonardo adjusted the loop around his head, which controlled the rudder section of the Great Bird, and he tested the hand cranks and foot stirrups, which raised and lowered the wings.

"Be careful," shouted Zoroastro, who had stepped back from the moving wings. "Are you trying to kill us?"

There was nervous laughter; but Leonardo was quiet. Achattabrigha tied the straps that would hold Leonardo fast to his machine and said, "I shall pray for your success, Leonardo, my son. I love you."

Leonardo turned to his step-father, smelled the good odors of Caterina's herbs—garlic and sweet onion—on his breath and clothes, and looked into the old man's squinting, pale blue eyes; and it came to him then, with the force of buried emotion, that he loved this man who had spent his life sweating by kiln fires and thinking with his great, yellow-nailed hands. "I love you, too... father. And I feel safe in your prayers."

That seemed to please Achattabrigha, for he checked the straps one last time, kissed Leonardo and patted his shoulder; then he stepped away, as reverently as if he were backing away from an icon in a cathedral.

"Good luck, Leonardo," Lorenzo said.

The others wished him luck. His father nodded, and smiled; and Leonardo, taking the weight of the Great Bird upon his back, lifted himself. Niccolò, Zoroastro, and Lorenzo de Credi helped him to the very edge of the ridge.

A cheer went up from below.

"Maestro, I wish it were me," Niccolò said. Tista stood beside him, looking longingly at Leonardo's flying mechanism.

"Just watch this time, Nicco," Leonardo said, and he nodded to Tista. "Pretend it is you who is flying in the heavens, for this machine is also yours. And you will be with me."

"Thank you, Leonardo."

"Now step away...for we must fly," Leonardo said; and he looked down, as if for the first time, as if every tree and upturned face were magnified; every smell, every sound and motion were clear and distinct. In some way the world had separated into its component elements, all in an instant; and in the distance, the swells and juttings of land were like that of a green sea with long, trailing shadows of brown; and upon those motionless waters were all the various constructions of human habitations: church and campanile, and shacks and barns and cottages and furrowed fields.

Leonardo felt sudden vertigo as his heart pounded in his chest. A breeze blew out of the northwest, and Leonardo felt it flow around him like a breath. The treetops rustled, whispering, as warm air drifted skyward. Thermal updrafts flowing invisibly to heaven. Pulling at him. His wings shuddered in the gusts; and Leonardo knew that it must be now, lest he be carried off the cliff unprepared.

He launched himself, pushing off the precipice as if he were diving from a cliff into the sea. For an instant, as he swooped downward, he felt euphoria. He was flying, carried by the wind, which embraced him in its cold grip. Then came heart-pounding, nauseating fear. Although he strained at the windlass and foot stirrups, which caused his great, fustian wings to flap, he could not keep himself aloft. His pushings and kickings had become almost reflexive from hours of practice: one leg thrust backward to lower one pair of wings while he furiously worked the windlass with his hands to raise the other, turning his hands first to the left, then to the right. He worked the mechanism with every bit of his calculated two hundred pound force, and his muscles ached from the strain. Although the Great Bird might function as a glider, there was too much friction in the gears to effect enough propulsive power; and the wind resistance was too strong. He could barely raise the wings.

He fell.

The chilling, cutting wind became a constant sighing in his ears. His clothes flapped against his skin like the fabric of his failing wings, while hills, sky, forest, and cliffs spiraled around him, then fell away; and he felt the damp shock of his recurring dream, his nightmare of falling into the void.

But he was falling through soft light, itself as tangible as butter. Below him was the familiar land of his youth, rising against all logic, rushing skyward to claim him. He could see his father's house and there in the distance the Apuan Alps and the ancient cobbled road built before Rome was an empire. His sensations took on the textures of dream; and he prayed, surprising himself, even then as he looked into the purple shadows of the impaling trees below. Still, he doggedly pedaled and turned the windlass mechanism.

All was calmness and quiet, but for the wind wheezing in his ears like the sea heard in a conch shell. His fear left him, carried away by the same breathing wind.

Then he felt a subtle bursting of warm air around him.

And suddenly, impossibly, vertiginously, he was ascending.

His wings were locked straight out. They were not flapping. Yet still he rose. It was as if God's hand were lifting Leonardo to Heaven; and he, Leonardo, remembered loosing his hawks into the air and watching them search for the currents of wind, which they used to soar into the highest of elevations, their wings motionless.

Thus did Leonardo rise in the warm air current—his mouth open to relieve the pressure constantly building in his ears—until he could see the top of the mountain... it was about a thousand feet below him. The country of hills and streams and farmland and forest had diminished, had become a neatly patterned board of swirls and rectangles: proof of man's work on earth. The sun seemed brighter at this elevation, as if the air itself was less dense in these attenuated regions. Leonardo feared now that he might be drawing too close to the region where air turned to fire.

He turned his head, pulling the loop that connected to the rudder; and found that he could, within bounds, control his direction. But then he stopped soaring; it was as if the warm bubble of air that had contained him had suddenly burst. He felt a chill.

The air became cold...and still.

He worked furiously at the windlass, thinking that he would beat his wings as birds do until they reach the wind; but he could not gain enough forward motion.

Once again, he fell like an arcing arrow.

Although the wind resistance was so great that he couldn't pull the wings below a horizontal position, he had developed enough speed to attain lift. He rose for a few beats, but, again, could not push his mechanism hard enough to maintain it, and another gust struck him, pummeling the Great Bird with phantomic fists.

Leonardo's only hope was to gain another warm thermal.

Instead, he became caught in a riptide of air that was like a blast, pushing the flying machine backward. He had all he could do to keep the wings locked in a horizontal position. He feared they might be torn away by the wind; and, indeed, the erratic gusts seemed to be conspiring to press him back down upon the stone face of the mountain.

Time seemed to slow for Leonardo; and in one long second he glimpsed the clearing surrounded by forest, as if forming a bull's-eye. He saw the tents and the townspeople who craned their necks to goggle up at him; and in this wind-wheezing moment, he suddenly gained a new, unfettered perspective. As if it were not he who was falling to his death.

Were his neighbors cheering? he wondered. Or were they horrified and dumbfounded at the sight of one of their own falling from the sky? More likely they were secretly wishing him to fall, their deepest desires not unlike the crowd that had recently cajoled a poor, love-sick peasant boy to jump from a rooftop onto the stone pavement of the Via Calimala.

The ground was now only three hundred feet below.

To his right, Leonardo caught sight of a hawk. The hawk was caught in the same trap of wind as Leonardo; and as he watched, the bird veered away, banking, and flew downwind. Leonardo shifted his weight, manipulated the rudder, and changed the angle of the wings. Thus he managed to follow the bird. His arms and legs felt like leaden weights, but he held on to his small measure of control.

Still he fell.

Two hundred feet.

He could hear the crowd shouting below him as clearly as if he were among them. People scattered, running to get out of Leonardo's way. He thought of his mother Caterina, for most men call upon their mothers at the moment of death.

And he followed the hawk, as if it were his inspiration, his own Beatrice.

And the ground swelled upward.

Then Leonardo felt as if he was suspended over the deep, green canopy of forest, but only for an instant. He felt a warm swell of wind; and the Great Bird rose, riding the thermal. Leonardo looked for the hawk, but it had disappeared as if it had been a spirit, rising without weight through the various spheres toward the *Primum Mobile.* He tried to control his flight, his thoughts toward landing in one of the fields beyond the trees.

The thermal carried him up; then, just as quickly, as if teasing him, burst. Leonardo tried to keep his wings fixed, and glided upwind for a few seconds. But a gust caught him, once again pushing him backward, and he fell—

Slapped back to earth.

Hubris.

I have come home to die.

His father's face scowled at him.

Leonardo had failed.

CHAPTER FIVE

Even after three weeks, the headaches remained.

Leonardo had suffered several broken ribs and a concussion when he fell into the forest, swooping between the thick, purple cypress trees, tearing like tissue the wood and fustaneum of the Great Bird's wings. His face was already turning black when Lorenzo's footmen found him. He recuperated at his father's home; but Lorenzo insisted on taking him to Villa Careggi, where he could have his physicians attend to him. With the exception of Lorenzo's personal dentator, who soaked a sponge in opium, morel juice, and hyoscyamus and extracted his broken tooth as Leonardo slept and dreamed of falling, they did little more than change his bandages, bleed him with leeches, and cast his horoscope.

Leonardo was more than relieved when the plague finally abated enough so that he could return to Florence. He was hailed as a hero, for Lorenzo had made a public announcement from the *ringhiera* of the Palazzo Vecchio that the artist from Vinci had, indeed, flown in the air like a bird. But the gossip among the educated was that, instead, Leonardo had fallen like

Icarus, whom it was said he resembled in *hubris*. He received an anonymous note that seemed to say it all: *victus honor.*

Honor to the vanquished.

Leonardo would accept none of the countless invitations to attend various masques and dinners and parties. He was caught up in a frenzy of work. He could not sleep; and when he would lose consciousness from sheer exhaustion, he would dream he was falling through the sky. He would see trees wheeling below him, twisting as if they were machines in an impossible torture chamber.

Leonardo was certain that the dreams would cease only when he conquered the air; and although he did not believe in ghosts or superstition, he was pursued by demons every bit as real as those conjured by the clergy he despised and mocked. So he worked, as if in a frenzy. He constructed new models and filled up three folios with his sketches and mirror-script notes. Niccolò and Tista would not leave him, except to bring him food, and Andrea Verrocchio came upstairs a few times a day to look in at his now famous apprentice.

"Haven't you yet had your bellyful of flying machines?" Andrea impatiently asked Leonardo. It was dusk, and dinner had already been served to the apprentices downstairs. Niccolò hurried to clear a place on the table so Andrea could put down the two bowls of boiled meat he had brought. Leonardo's studio was in its usual state of disarray, but the old flying machine, the insects mounted on boards, the vivisected birds and bats, the variously designed wings, rudders, and valves for the Great Bird were gone, replaced by new drawings, new mechanisms for testing wing designs (for now the wings would remain fixed), and various large-scale models of free-flying whirlybird toys, which had been in use since the 1300s. He was experimenting with inverted cones—Archimedian Screws—to cheat gravity, and he studied the geometry of children's tops to calculate the principle of the fly-wheel. Just as a ruler whirled rapidly in the air will guide the arm by the line of the edge of the flat surface, so did Leonardo envision a machine powered by a flying propeller. Yet he could not help but think that such mechanisms were against nature, for air was a fluid, like water. And nature, the protoplast of all man's creation, had not invented rotary motion.

Leonardo pulled the string of a toy whirlybird, and the tiny four-bladed propeller spun into the air, as if in defiance of all natural laws. "No, Andrea, I have not lost my interest in this most sublime of inventions. *Il Magnifico* has listened to my ideas, and he is enthusiastic that my next machine will remain aloft."

Verrocchio watched the red propeller glide sideways into a stack of books: *De Onesta Volutta* by Il Platina, the *Letters of Filefo*, Pliny's *Historia naturale*, Dati's *Trattato della sfera*, and Ugo Benzo's *On the Preservation of the Health*. "And Lorenzo has offered to recompense you for these...experiments?"

"Such an invention would revolutionize the very nature of warfare," Leonardo insisted. "I've developed an exploding missile that looks like a dart and could be dropped from my Great Bird. I've also been experimenting with improvements on the arquebus, and I have a design for a giant *ballista*, a cross-bow of a kind never before imagined. I've designed a cannon with many racks of barrels that—"

"Indeed," Verrocchio said. "But I have advised you that it is unwise to put your trust in Lorenzo's momentary enthusiasms."

"Certainly the First Citizen has more than a passing interest in armaments."

"Is that why he ignored your previous memorandum wherein you proposed the very same ideas?"

"That was before, and this is now."

"Ah, certainly," Andrea said, nodding his head. Then after a pause, he said, "Stop this foolishness, Leonardo. You're a painter, and a painter should paint. "Why have you been unwilling to work on any of the commissions I have offered you? And you've refused many other good offers. You have no money, and you've gained yourself a bad reputation."

"I will have more than enough money after the world watches my flying machine soar into the heavens."

"You are lucky to be alive, Leonardo. Have you not looked at yourself in a mirror? And you nearly broke your spine. Are you so intent upon doing so again? Or will killing yourself suffice?" He shook his head, as if angry at himself. " You've become skinny as a rail and sallow as an old man. Do you eat what we bring you? Do you sleep?" Do you *paint*? No, nothing but invention, nothing but...this." He waved his arm at the models and mechanisms that lay everywhere. Then in a soft voice, he said, "I blame myself. I should have never allowed you to proceed with all this in the first place. You need a strong hand."

"When Lorenzo sees what I have—"

Andrea made a tssing sound by tapping the roof of his mouth with his tongue. "I bid thee goodnight. Leonardo, eat your food before it gets cold. Niccolò, see that he eats."

"Andrea?" Leonardo said.

"Yes?"

"What has turned you against me?

"My love for you... Forget invention and munitions and flying toys. You are a painter. Paint."

"I cannot," Leonardo answered, but in a voice so low that no one else could hear.

CHAPTER SIX

"Stop it, that hurts!" Tista said to Niccolò, who had pulled him away from Leonardo's newest flying machine and held his arm behind him, as if to break it.

"Do you promise to stay away from the Maestro's machine?" Niccolò asked.

"Yes, I promise."

Niccolò let go of the boy, who backed nervously away from him. Leonardo stood a few paces away, oblivious to them, and stared down the mountain side to the valley below. Mist flowed dreamlike down its grassy slopes; in the distance, surrounded by grayish-green hills, was Florence, its Duomo and the high tower of the Palazzo Vecchio golden in the early sunlight. It was a brisk morning in early March, but it would be a warm day. The vapor from Leonardo's exhalations was faint. He had come here to test his glider, which now lay nearby, its large, arched wings lashed to the ground. Leonardo had taken Niccolò's advice. This flying machine had fixed wings and no motor. It was a glider. His plan was to master flight; when he developed a suitable engine to power his craft, he would then know how to control it. And this machine was more in keeping with Leonardo's ideas of nature, for he would wear the wings, as if he were, indeed, a bird; he would hang from the wings, legs below, head and shoulders above, and control them by swinging his legs and shifting his weight. He would be like a bird soaring, sailing, gliding.

But he had put off flying the contraption for the last two days that they had camped here. Even though he was certain that its design was correct, he had lost his nerve. He was afraid. He just could not do it.

But he had to...

He could feel Niccolò and Tista watching him.

He kicked at some loamy dirt and decided: he would do it now. He would not think about it. If he was to die...then so be it. Could being a coward be worse than falling out of the sky?

But he was too late, too late by a breath.

Niccolò shouted.

Startled, Leonardo turned to see that Tista had torn loose the rope that anchored the glider to the ground and had pulled himself through the opening between the wings. Leonardo shouted "stop" and rushed toward him, but Tista threw himself over the crest before either Leonardo or Niccolò could stop him. In fact, Leonardo had to grab Niccolò, who almost fell from the mountain in pursuit of his friend.

Tista's cry carried through the chill, thin air, but it was a cry of joy as the boy soared through the empty sky. He circled the mountain, catching the warmer columns of air, and then descended.

"Come back," Leonardo shouted through cupped hands, yet he could not help but feel an exhilaration, a thrill. The machine worked! But it was he, Leonardo, who needed to be in the air.

"Maestro, I tried to stop him," Niccolò cried.

But Leonardo ignored him, for the weather suddenly changed, and buffeting wind began to whip around the mountain. "Stay away from the slope," Leonardo called. But he could not be heard; and he watched helplessly as the glider pitched upwards, caught by a gust. It stalled in the chilly air, and then fell like a leaf. "Swing your hips forward," Leonardo shouted. The glider could be brought under control. If the boy was practiced, it would not be difficult at all. But he wasn't, and the glider slid sideways, crashing into the mountain.

Niccolò screamed, and Leonardo discovered that he, too, was screaming.

Tista was tossed out of the harness. Grabbing at brush and rocks, he fell about fifty feet.

By the time Leonardo reached him, the boy was almost unconscious. He lay between two jagged rocks, his head thrown back, his back twisted, arms and legs akimbo.

"Where do you feel pain?" Leonardo asked as he tried to make the boy as comfortable as he could. There was not much that could be done, for Tista's back was broken, and a rib had pierced the skin. Niccolò kneeled beside Tista; his face was white, as if drained of blood.

"I feel no pain, Maestro. Please do not be angry with

me." Niccolò took his hand.

"I am not angry, Tista. But why did you do it?"

"I dreamed every night that I was flying. In your contraption, Leonardo. The very one. I could not help myself. I planned how I would do it." He smiled wanly. "And I did it."

"That you did," whispered Leonardo, remembering his own dream of falling. Could one dreamer effect another?

"Niccolò...?" Tista called in barely a whisper.

"I am here."

"I cannot see very well. I see the sky, I think."

Niccolò looked to Leonardo, who could only shake his head.

When Tista shuddered and died, Niccolò began to cry and beat his hands against the sharp rocks, bloodying them. Leonardo embraced him, holding his arms tightly and rocking him back and forth as if he were a baby. All the while he did so, he felt revulsion; for he could not help himself, he could not control his thoughts, which were as hard and cold as reason itself.

Although his flying machine had worked—or would have worked successfully, if he, Leonardo, had taken it into the air—he had another idea for a great bird.

One that would be safe.

As young Tista's inchoate soul rose to the heavens like a kite in the wind, Leonardo imagined just such a machine.

A child's kite...

* * * * * * *

"So it is true, you are painting," Andrea Verrochio said, as he stood in Leonardo's studio. Behind him stood Niccolò and Sandro Botticelli.

Although the room was still cluttered with his various instruments and machines and models, the tables had been cleared, and the desiccated corpses of birds and animals and insects were gone. The ripe odors of rot were replaced with the raw, pungent fumes of linseed oil and varnish and paint. Oil lamps inside globes filled with water—another of Leonardo's inventions—cast cones of light in the cavernous room; he had surrounded himself and his easel with the brightest of these watery lamps, which created a room of light within the larger room that seemed to be but mere appearance.

"But what kind of painting is this?" Andrea asked. "Did the Anti-Christ need to decorate the dark walls of his church? I could believe that only he could commission such work"

Leonardo grimaced and cast an angry look at Niccolò for bringing company into his room when he was working. Since Tista had died, he had taken to sleeping during the day and painting all night. He turned to Verrochio. "I'm only following your advice, Maestro. You said that a painter paints."

"Indeed, I did. But a painter does not paint for himself, in the darkness, as you are doing"; yet even as he spoke, he leaned toward the large canvass Leonardo was working on, casting his shadow over a third of it. He seemed fascinated with the central figure of a struggling man being carried into Hell by the monster Geryon; man and beast were painted with such depth and precision that they looked like tiny live figures trapped in amber. The perspective of the painting was dizzying, for it was a glimpse into the endless shafts and catacombs of Hell; indeed, Paolo Ucello, may he rest in peace, would have been proud of such work, for he had lived for the beauties of perspective.

"Leonardo, I have called upon you twice...why did you turn me away?" Sandro asked. "And why have you not responded to any of my letters?" He looked like a younger version of Master Andrea, for he had the same kind of wide, fleshy face, but Botticelli's jaw was stronger; and while Verrocchio's lips were thin and tight, Sandro's were heavy and sensuous.

"I have not received anyone," Leonardo said, stepping out of the circle of light. Since Tista was buried, his only company was Niccolò, who would not leave his master.

"And neither have you responded to the invitations of the First Citizen," Verrocchio said, meaning Lorenzo de Medici.

"Is that why you're here?" Leonardo asked Sandro. Even in the lamplight, he could see a blush in his friend's cheeks, for he was part of the Medici family; Lorenzo loved him as he did his own brother, Giuliano.

"I'm here because I'm worried about *you*, as is Lorenzo. You have done the same for me, or have you forgotten?"

No, Leonardo had not forgotten. He remembered

when Sandro had almost died of love for Lorenzo's mistress, Simonetta Vespucci. He remembered how Sandro had lost weight and dreamed even when he was awake; how Pico Della Mirandola had exorcised him in the presence of Simonetta and Lorenzo; and how he, Leonardo, had taken care of him until he regained his health.

"So you think I am in need of Messer Mirandola's services?" Leonardo asked. "Is that it?"

"I think you need to see your friends. I think you need to come awake in the light and sleep in the night. I think you must stop grieving for the child Tista."

Leonardo was about to respond, but caught himself. He wasn't grieving for Tista. Niccolò was, certainly. He, Leonardo, was simply working.

Working through his fear and guilt and...

Grief.

For it was, somehow, as if *he* had fallen and broken his spine, as, perhaps, he should have when he fell from the mountain ledge as a child.

"Leonardo, why are you afraid?" Niccolò asked. "The machine...worked. It *will* fly."

"And so you wish to fly it, too? Leonardo asked, but it was more a statement than a question; he was embarrassed and vexed that Niccolò would demean him in front of Verrochio.

But, indeed, the machine had worked.

"I am going back to bed," Verrochio said, bowing to Sandro. "I will leave you to try to talk sense into my apprentice." He looked at Leonardo and smiled, for both knew that he was an apprentice in name only. But Leonardo would soon have to earn his keep; for Verrochio's patience was coming to an end. He gazed at Leonardo's painting. "You know, the good monks of St. Bernard might just be interested in such work as this. Perhaps I might suggest that they take your painting instead of the altarpiece you owe them."

Leonardo could not help but laugh, for he knew that his master was serious.

After Verrochio left, Leonardo and Sandro sat down on a cassone together under one of the dirty high windows of the studio; Niccolò sat before them on the floor; he was all eyes and ears and attention.

"Nicco, bring us some wine," Leonardo said.

"I want to be *here*."

Leonardo did not argue with the boy. It was unimportant, and once the words were spoken, forgotten. Leonardo gazed upward. He could see the sky through the window; the stars were brilliant, for Florence was asleep and its lanterns did not compete with the stars. "I thought I could get so close to them," he said, as if talking to himself. He imagined the stars as tiny pricks in the heavenly fabric; he could even now feel the heat from the region of fire held at bay by the darkness; and as if he could truly see through imagination, he watched himself soaring in his flying machine, climbing into the black heavens, soaring, reaching to burn like paper for one glorious instant into those hot, airy regions above the clouds and night.

But this flying machine he imagined was like no

other device he had ever sketched or built. He had reached beyond nature to conceive a child's kite with flat surfaces to support it in the still air. Like his dragonfly contraption, it would have double wings, cellular open-ended boxes that would be as stable as kites of like construction.

Stable...and safe.

The pilot would not need to shift his balance to keep control. He would float on the air like a raft. Tista would not have lost his balance and fallen out of the sky in this contraption.

"Leonardo...*Leonardo*! Have you been listening to anything I've said?"

"Yes, Little Bottle, I hear you." Leonardo was one of a very small circle of friends who was permitted to call Sandro by his childhood nickname.

"Then I can tell Lorenzo that you will demonstrate your new flying machine? It would not be wise to refuse him, Leonardo. He has finally taken notice of you. He needs you now; his enemies are everywhere."

Leonardo nodded.

Indeed, the First Citizen's relationship with the ambitious Pope Sixtus IV was at a breaking-point, and all of Florence lived in fear of excommunication and war.

"Florence must show it's enemies that it is invincible," Sandro continued. "A device that can rain fire from the sky would deter even the Pope."

"I knew that Lorenzo could not long ignore my inventions," Leonardo said, although he was surprised.

"He plans to elevate you to the position of master of

engines and captain of engineers."

"Should I thank you for this, Little Bottle?" Leonardo asked. "Lorenzo would have no reason to think that my device would work. Rather the opposite, as it killed my young apprentice."

"God rest his soul," Sandro said.

Leonardo continued. "Unless someone whispered in Lorenzo's ear. I fear you have gone from being artist to courtier, Little Bottle."

"The honors go to Niccolò," Sandro said. "It is he who convinced Lorenzo."

"This is what you've been waiting for, Maestro," Niccolò said. "I will find Francesco at first light and tell him to help you build another Great Bird. And I'll get the wine right now."

"Wait a moment," Leonardo said, then directed himself to Sandro. "How did Nicco convince Lorenzo?"

"You sent me with a note for the First Citizen, Maestro, when you couldn't accept his invitation to attend Simonetta's ball," Niccolò said. "I told him of our grief over Tista, and then I also had to explain what had happened. Although I loved Tista, he was at fault. Not our machine... Lorenzo understood."

"Ah, did he now."

"I only did as you asked," Niccolò insisted.

"And did you speak to him about my bombs?" Leonardo asked.

"Yes, Maestro."

"And did he ask you, or did you volunteer that information?

Niccolò glanced nervously at Sandro, as if he would supply him with the answer. "I thought you would be pleased..."

"I think you may get the wine now, Sandro said to Niccolò, who did not miss the opportunity to flee. Then he directed himself to Leonardo. "You should have congratulated Niccolò, not berated him. Why were you so hard on the boy?"

Leonardo gazed across the room at his painting in the circle of lamps. He desired only to paint, not construct machines to kill children; he would paint his dreams, which had fouled his waking life with their strength and startling detail. By painting them, by exposing them, he might free himself. Yet ideas for his great Kite seemed to appear like chiaroscuro on the painting of his dream of falling, as if it were a notebook.

Leonardo shivered, for his dreams had spilled out of his sleep and would not let him go. Tonight they demanded to be painted.

Tomorrow they would demand to be built.

He yearned to step into the cold, perfect spaces of his memory cathedral, which had become his haven. There he could imagine each painting, each dream, and lock it in its own dark, private room. As if every experience, every pain, could be so isolated.

"Well...?" Sandro asked.

"I will apologize to Niccolò when he returns," Leonardo said.

"Leonardo, was Niccolò right? Are you afraid? I'm your best friend, certainly you can—"

Just then Niccolò appeared with a bottle of wine.

"I am very tired, Little Bottle," Leonardo said. "Perhaps we can celebrate another day. I will take your advice and sleep...to come awake in the light."

That was, of course, a lie, for Leonardo painted all night and the next day. It was as if he had to complete a month's worth of ideas in a few hours. Ideas seemed to explode in his mind's eye, paintings complete; all that Leonardo had to do was trace them onto canvass and mix his colors. It was as if he had somehow managed to unlock doors in his memory cathedral and glimpse what St. Augustine had called the present of things future; it was as if he were glimpsing ideas he *would* have, paintings he *would* paint; and he knew that if he didn't capture these gifts now, he would lose them forever. Indeed, it was as if he were dreaming whilst awake, and during these hours, whether awake or slumped over before the canvass in a catnap or a trance, he had no control over the images that glowed in his mind like the lanterns placed on the floor, cassones, desks, and tables around him, rings of light, as if everything was but different aspects of Leonardo's dream...Leonardo's conception. He worked in a frenzy, which was always how he worked when his ideas caught fire; but this time he had no conscious focus or goal. Rather than a frenzy of discovery, this was a kind of remembering.

By morning he had six paintings under way; one was a Madonna, transcendantly radiant, as if Leonardo had lifted the veil of human sight to reveal the divine substance. The others seemed to be grotesque visions of hell that would only be matched by a young Dutch contemporary of Leonardo's: Hieronoymus Bosh. There was a savage cruelty in these pictures of fabulous monsters with gnashing snouts, bat's wings, crocodile's jaws, and scaly pincered tails, yet every creature, every caricature and grotesquerie had a single haunting human feature: chimeras with soft, sad human eyes or womanly limbs or the angelic faces of children taunting and torturing the fallen in the steep, dark mountainous wastes of Hell.

As promised, Niccolò fetched Verrocchio's foreman Francesco to supervise the rebuilding of Leonardo's flying machine; but not at first light, as he had promised, for the exhausted Niccolò had slept until noon. Leonardo had thought that Niccolò was cured of acting independently on his master's behalf; but obviously the boy was not contrite, for he had told Leonardo that he was going downstairs to bring back some meat and fruit for lunch.

But Leonardo surprised both of them by producing a folio of sketches, diagrams, plans, and design measurements for kites and two and three winged soaring machines. Some had curved surfaces, some had flat surfaces; but all these drawings and diagrams were based on the idea of open ended boxes...groups of them placed at the ends of timber spars. There were detailed diagrams of triplane and biplane gliders with wing span and supporting surface measurements; even on paper these machines looked awkward and heavy and bulky, for they did not imitate nature. He had tried imitation, but nature was capricious, unmanageable. Now he would conquer it. *Vince la natura.* Not even Tista could fall from these rectangular rafts. Leonardo had scribbled notes below two sketches of cellular kites, but not in his backward script; this was obviously meant to be readable to others: *Determine whether kite with cambered wings will travel farther. Fire from crossbow to ensure accuracy.* And on another page, a sketch of three kites flying in tandem, one above the other, and below a figure on a sling seat: *Total area of surface sails 476 ells. Add kites with sails of 66 ells to compensate for body weight over 198 pounds. Shelter from wind during assembly, open kites one at a time, then pull away supports to allow the wind to get under the sails. Tether the last kite, lest you be carried away.*

"Can you produce these kites for me by tomorrow?" Leonardo asked Francesco, as he pointed to the sketch. I've provided all the dimensions."

"Impossible," Francesco said. "Perhaps when your flying machine for the First Citizen is finished—"

"This *will* be for the First Citizen," Leonardo insisted.

"I was instructed to rebuild the flying machine in which young Tista was...in which he suffered his accident."

"By whom? Niccolò?

"Leonardo, Maestro Andrea has interrupted work on the altarpiece for the Chapel of Saint Bernard to build your contraption for the First Citizen. When that's completed, I'll help you build these...kites."

Leonardo knew Francesco well; he wouldn't get

anywhere by cajoling him. He nodded and sat down before the painting of a Madonna holding the Child, who, in turn, was holding a cat. The painting seemed to be movement itself.

"Don't you wish to supervise the work, Maestro?" asked the foreman.

"No, I'll begin constructing the kites, with Niccolò."

"Maestro, Lorenzo expects us—you—to demonstrate your Great Bird in a fortnight. You and Sandro agreed."

"Sandro is not the First Citizen." Then after a pause, "I have better ideas for soaring machines."

"But they cannot be built in time, Maestro," Niccolò insisted.

"Then no machine will be built."

And with that, Leonardo went back to his painting of the Madonna, which bore a sensual resemblance to Lorenzo's mistress Simonetta.

Which would be a gift for Lorenzo.

CHAPTER SEVEN

After a short burst of pelting rain, steady winds seemed to cleanse the sky of the gray storm clouds that had suffocated the city for several days in an atmospheric inversion. It had also been humid, and the air, which tasted dirty, had made breathing difficult. Florentine citizens closed their shutters against the poisonous miasmas, which were currently thought to be the cause of the deadly buboes, and were, at the very least, ill omens. But Leonardo, who had finally completed building his tandem kites after testing design after design, did not even know that a disaster had befallen Verrochio's bottega when rotten timbers in the roof gave way during the storm. He and Niccolò had left to test the kites in a farmer's field nestled in a windy valley that also afforded privacy. As Leonardo did not want Zoroastro or Lorenzo de Credi, or anyone else along, he designed a sled so he could haul his lightweight materials himself.

"Maestro, are you going to make your peace with Master Andrea?" Niccolò asked as they waited for the mid-morning winds, which were the strongest. The sky was clear and soft and gauzy blue, a peculiar atmospheric effect seen only in Tuscany; Leonardo had been told that in other places, especially to the north, the sky was sharper, harder.

"I will soon start a bottega of my own," Leonardo said, "and be the ruler of my own house."

"But we need money, Maestro."

"We'll have it."

"Not if you keep the First Citizen waiting for his Great Bird," Niccolò said; and Leonardo noticed that the boy's eyes narrowed, as if he were calculating a mathematical problem. "Maestro Andrea will certainly have to tell Lorenzo that your Great Bird is completed."

"Has he done so?" Leonardo asked.

Niccolò shrugged.

"He will be even more impressed with my new invention. I will show him before he becomes too impatient. But I think it is Andrea, not Lorenzo, who is impatient."

"You're going to show the First Citizen *this*?" Niccolò asked, meaning the tandem kites, which were protected from any gusts of wind by a secured canvass; the kites were assembled, and when Leonardo was ready, would be opened one at a time.

"If this works, then we will build the Great Bird as I promised. That will buy us our bottega and Lorenzo's love."

"He loves you already, Maestro, as does Maestro Andrea."

"Then they'll be patient with me."

Niccolò was certainly not above arguing with his

master; he had, indeed, become Leonardo's confidant. But Leonardo didn't give him a chance. He had been checking the wind, which would soon be high. "Come help me, Nicco, and try not to be a philosopher. The wind is strong enough. If we wait it will become too gusty and tear the kites." This had already happened to several of Leonardo's large scale models.

Leonardo let the wind take the first and smallest of the kites, but the wind was rather puffy, and it took a few moments before it pulled its thirty pounds on the guy rope. Then, as the wind freshened, he let go another. Satisfied, he anchored the assembly, making doubly sure that it was secure, and opened the third and largest kite. "Hold the line tight," he said to Niccolò as he climbed onto the sling seat and held tightly to a restraining rope that ran through a block and tackle to a makeshift anchor of rocks.

Leonardo reassured himself that he was safely tethered and reminded himself that the cellular box was the most stable of constructions. Its flat surfaces would support it in the air. Nevertheless, his heart seemed to be pulsing in his throat, he had difficulty taking a breath, and he could feel the chill of his sweat on his chest and arms.

The winds were strong, but erratic, and Leonardo waited until he could feel the wind pulling steady; he leaned backward, sliding leeward on the seat to help the wind get under the supporting surface of the largest kite. Then suddenly, as if some great heavenly hand had grabbed hold of the guy ropes and the kites and snapped them, Leonardo shot upward about twenty feet. But the kites held steady at the end of their tether, floating on the wind like rafts on water.

How different this was from the Great Bird, which was so sensitive—and susceptible—to every movement of the body. Leonardo shifted his weight, and even as he did so, he prayed; but the kites held in the air. Indeed, they were rafts. The answer was ample supporting surfaces.

Vince la natura.

The wind lightened, and he came down. The kites dragged him forward; he danced along the ground on his toes before he was swept upwards again. Niccolò was shouting, screaming, and hanging from the restraining rope, as if to add his weight, lest it pull away from the rock anchor or pull the rocks heavenward.

When the kites came down for the third time, Leonardo jumped from the sling seat, falling to the ground. Seconds later, as if slapped by he same hand that had pulled them into the sky, the kites crashed, splintering, as their sails snapped and fluttered, as if still yearning for the airy heights.

"Are you all right, Maestro," Niccolò shouted, running toward Leonardo.

"Yes," Leonardo said, although his back was throbbing in pain and his right arm, which he had already broken once before, was numb. But he could move it, as well as all his fingers. "I'm fine." He surveyed the damage. "Let's salvage what we can."

They fastened the broken kites onto the sled and

walked through wildflower dotted fields and pastures back to the bottega. "Perhaps now, Maestro, you'll trust your original Great Bird," Niccolò said. "You mustn't bury it with Tista."

"What are you talking about?" Leonardo asked.

"These kites are too...dangerous. They're completely at the mercy of the wind; they dragged you along the ground; and you almost broke your arm. Isn't that right, Maestro?"

Leonardo detected a touch of irony in Niccolò's voice. So the boy was having it up on his master. "Yes," Leonardo said. "And what does that prove?"

"That you should give this up."

"On the contrary, Nicco. This experiment has only proved how safe my new Great Bird will be."

"But you—"

Leonardo showed Niccolò his latest drawing of a biplane based on his idea of open ended boxes placed at the ends of timber spars.

"How could such a thing fly?" Niccolò asked.

"That's a soaring machine safe enough for Lorenzo himself. If I could show the First Citizen that he could command the very air, do you think he would regret the few days it will take to build and test the new machine?"

"I think it looks very dangerous...and I think the kites are very dangerous, Maestro."

Leonardo smiled at Niccolò. "Then at least after today you no longer think I am a coward."

"Maestro, I *never* thought that."

But even as they approached the city, Leonardo could feel the edges of his dream, the dark edges of nightmare lingering; and he knew that tonight it would return.

The dream of falling. The dream of flight.

Tista...

He would stay up and work. He would not sleep. He would not dream. But the dream spoke to him even as he walked, told him *it* was nature and would not be conquered. And Leonardo could feel himself

Falling.

* * * * * * *

If Leonardo were superstitious, he would have believed it was a sign.

When the roof of Verrochio's bottega gave way, falling timber and debris destroyed almost everything in Leonardo's studio; and the pelting rain ruined most of what might have been salvaged. Leonardo could rewrite his notes, for they were safe in the altar of his memory cathedral; he could rebuild models and replenish supplies, but his painting of the Madonna— his gift for Lorenzo—was destroyed. The canvass torn, the oils smeared, and the still-sticky varnish surface spackled with grit and filth. Most everything but the three paintings of his nightmare-descent into Hell was destroyed. They were placed against the inner wall of the studio, a triptych of dark canvasses, exposed, the varnish still sticky, protected by a roll of fabric that had fallen over them. And in every one of them Leonardo could see himself as a falling or fallen figure.

The present of the future.

"Don't you think this is a sign from the gods?" Niccolò asked after he and Leonardo had salvaged what they could and moved into another studio in Verrochio's bottega.

"Do you now believe in the Greek's pantheon?" Leonardo asked.

Looking flustered, Niccolò said, "I only meant—"

"I know what you meant." Leonardo smiled tightly. "Maestro Andrea might get his wish...he might yet sell those paintings to the good monks. In the meantime, we've got work to do, which we'll start at first light."

"We can't build your Great Bird alone," Niccolò insisted.

"Of course we can. And Francesco will allocate some of his apprentices to help us."

"Maestro Andrea won't allow it."

"We'll see," Leonardo said.

"Maestro, your Great Bird is *already* built. It is ready, and Lorenzo expects you to fly it."

"Would that the roof fell upon it." Leonardo gazed out the window into the streets. The full moon illuminated the houses and bottegas and shops and palazzos in weak gray light that seemed to be made brighter by the yellow lamplight trembling behind vellum covered windows. He would make Lorenzo a model of his new soaring machine, his new Great Bird; but he would not see the First Citizen until it was built and tested. Indeed, he stayed up the night redrawing his designs, reworking his ideas, as if the destruction of his studio had been a blessing. He sketched cellular box kite designs that he combined into new forms for gliding machines, finally settling on a design based almost entirely on the rectangular box kite forms. He had broken away from the natural bird-like forms, yet this device was not unnatural in its simplicity. He detailed crosshatch timber braces, which would keep his cellular wing surfaces tight. He made drawings and diagrams of the cordage. The pilot would sit in a sling below the double wings, which were webbed as the masts of a sailing vessel; and the rudder would be attached to long spars that stretched behind him at shoulder height. A ship to sail into the heavens.

Tomorrow he would build models to test his design. To his mind, the ship was already built, for it was as tangible as the notebook he was staring into.

Notebook in hand, he fell asleep, for he had been little removed from dreams; and dream he did, dreams as textured and deep and tinted as memory. He rode his Great Bird through the moonlit night, sailed around the peaks of mountains as if they were islands in a calm, warm sea; and the winds carried him, carried him away into darkness, into the surfaces of his paintings that had survived the rain and roof, into the brushstroked chiaroscuro of his imagined hell.

CHAPTER EIGHT

"Tell Lorenzo that I'll have a soaring machine ready to impress the archbishop when he arrives," Leonardo said. "But he's not due for a fortnight."

"You've taken too long already." Sandro Botticelli stood in Leonardo's new studio, which was small and in disarray; although the roof had been repaired, Leonardo did not want to waste time moving back into his old room. Sandro was dressed as a dandy, in red and green, with dags and a peaked cap pulled over his thick brown hair. It was a festival day, and the Medici and their retinue would take to the streets for the Palio, the great annual horse race. "Lorenzo sent me to drag you to the Palio, if need be."

"If Andrea had allowed Francesco to help me—or at least lent me a few apprentices—I would have it finished by now."

"That's not the point."

"That's exactly the point."

"Get out of your smock; you must have something that's not covered with paint and dirt."

"Come, I'll show you what I've done," Leonardo said. "I've put up canvass outside to work on my soaring machine. It's like nothing you've ever seen, I promise you that. I'll call Niccolò, he'll be happy to see you."

"You can show it to me on our way, Leonardo. Now get dressed. Niccolò has left long ago."

"What?"

"Have you lost touch with everyone and everything?" Sandro asked. "Niccolò is at the Palio with Andrea... who is with Lorenzo. Only you remain behind."

"But Niccolò was just here."

Sandro shook his head. "He's been there for most of the day. He said he begged you to accompany him."

"Did he tell that to Lorenzo, too?"

"I think you can trust your young apprentice to be discreet."

Dizzy with fatigue, Leonardo sat down by a table covered with books and models of kites and various incarnations of his soaring machine. "Yes, of course, you're right, Little Bottle."

"You look like you've been on a binge. You've got to start taking care of yourself, you've got to start sleeping and eating properly. If you don't, you'll lose everything, including Lorenzo's love and attention. You can't treat him as you do the rest of your friends. I thought you wanted to be his master of engineers."

"What else has Niccolò been telling you?"

Sandro shook his head in a gesture of exasperation, and said, "Change your clothes, dear friend. We haven't more than an hour before the race begins."

"I'm not going," Leonardo said, his voice flat. "Lorenzo will have to wait until my soaring machine is ready."

"He will not wait."

"He has no choice."

"He has your Great Bird, Leonardo."

"Then Lorenzo can fly it. Perhaps he will suffer the same fate as Tista. Better yet, he should order Andrea to fly it. After all, Andrea had it built for him."

"Leonardo..."

"It killed Tista... It's not safe."

"I'll tell Lorenzo you're ill," Sandro said.

"Send Niccolò back to me. I forbid him to—"

But Sandro had already left the studio, closing the large inlaid door behind him.

Exhausted, Leonardo leaned upon the table and imagined that he had followed Sandro to the door, down the stairs, and outside. There he surveyed his canvass-covered makeshift workshop. The air was hot and stale in the enclosed space. It would take weeks working alone to complete the new soaring machine. Niccolò should be here. Then Leonardo began working at the cordage to tighten the supporting wing surfaces. *This* machine will be safe, he thought; and he worked, even in the dark exhaustion of his dreams, for he had lost the ability to rest.

Indeed he was lost.

In the distance he could hear Tista. Could hear the boy's triumphant cry before he fell and snapped his spine. And he heard thunder. Was it the shouting of the crowd as he, Leonardo, fell from the mountain near Vinci? Was it the crowd cheering the Palio riders racing through the city? Or was it the sound of his own dream-choked breathing?

* * * * * * *

"Leonardo, they're going to fly your machine."

"What?" Leonardo asked, surfacing from deep sleep; his head ached and his limbs felt weak and light, as if he had been carrying heavy weights.

Francesco stood over him, and Leonardo could smell the man's sweat and the faint odor of garlic. "One of my boys came back to tell me...as if *I'd* be rushing into crowds of cutpurses to see some child die in your flying contraption." He took a breath, catching himself. "I'm sorry, Maestro. Don't take offense, but you know what I think of your machines."

"Lorenzo is going to demonstrate my Great Bird *now*?"

Francesco shrugged. "After his brother won the Palio, *Il Magnifico* announced to the crowds that an angel would fly above them and drop Hell's own fire from the sky. And my apprentice tells me that *inquisitore* are all over the streets and are keeping everyone away from the gardens near *Santi Apostoli*."

That would certainly send a message to the Pope; the church of *Santi Apostoli* was under the protection of the powerful Pazzi family, who were allies of Pope Sixtus and enemies of the Medici.

"When is this supposed to happen?" Leonardo asked the foreman as he hurriedly put on a new shirt; a doublet; and *calze* hose, which were little more than pieces of leather to protect his feet.

Francesco shrugged. "I came to tell you as soon as I heard."

"And did you hear who is to fly my machine?"

"I've told you all I know, Maestro." Then after a pause, he said, "But I fear for Niccolò. I fear he has told *Il Magnifico* that he knows how to fly your inventions."

Leonardo prayed he could find Niccolò before he came to harm. He too feared that the boy had betrayed him, had insinuated himself into Lorenzo's confidence, and was at this moment soaring over Florence in the Great Bird. Soaring over the Duomo, the Baptistry, and the Piazza della Signoria, which rose from the streets like minarets around a heavenly dome.

But the air currents over Florence were too dangerous. He would fall like Tista, for what was the city but a mass of jagged peaks and precipitous cliffs.

"Thank you, Francesco," Leonardo said, and, losing no time, he made his way through the crowds toward the church of *Santi Apostoli*. A myriad of smells delicious and noxious permeated the air: roasting meats, honeysuckle, the odor of candle wax heavy as if with childhood memories, offal and piss, cattle and horses, the tang of wine and cider, and everywhere sweat and the sour ripe scent of perfumes applied to unclean bodies. The shouting and laughter and stepping-rushing-soughing of the crowds were deafening, as if a human tidal wave was making itself felt across the city. The whores were out in full regalia, having left their district which lay between Santa Giovanni and

Santa Maria Maggiore; they worked their way through the crowds, as did the cutpurses and pickpockets, the children of Firenze's streets. Beggars grasped onto visiting country villeins and minor guildesmen for a denari and saluted when the red *carroccios* with their long scarlet banners and red, dressed horses passed. Merchants and bankers and wealthy guildesmen rode on great horses or were comfortable in their carriages, while their servants walked ahead to clear the way for them with threats and brutal proddings.

The frantic, noisy streets mirrored Leonardo's frenetic inner state, for he feared for Niccolò; and he walked quickly, his hand openly resting on the hilt of his razor-sharp dagger to deter thieves and those who would slice open the belly of a passer-by for amusement.

He kept looking for likely places from which his Great Bird might be launched: the dome of the Duomo, high brick towers, the roof of the Baptistry...and he looked up at the darkening sky, looking for his Great Bird as he pushed his way through the crowds to the gardens near the Santi Apostoli, which was near the Ponte Vecchio. In these last few moments, Leonardo became hopeful. Perhaps there was a chance to stop Niccolò...if, indeed, Niccolò was to fly the Great Bird for Lorenzo.

Blocking entry to the gardens were both Medici and Pazzi supporters, two armies, dangerous and armed, facing each other. Lances and swords flashed in the dusty twilight. Leonardo could see the patriarch of the

Pazzi family, the shrewd and haughty Jacopo de' Pazzi, an old, full-bodied man sitting erect on a huge, richly carapaced charger, His sons Giovanni, Francesco, and Guglielmo were beside him, surrounded by their troops dressed in the Pazzi colors of blue and gold. And there, to Leonardo's surprise and frustration, was his great Eminence the Archbishop, protected by the scions of the Pazzi family and their liveried guards. So this was why Lorenzo had made his proclamation that he would conjure an angel of death and fire to demonstrate the power of the Medici...and Florence. It was as if the Pope himself were here to watch.

Beside the Archbishop, in dangerous proximity to the Pazzi, Lorenzo and Giuliano sat atop their horses. Giuliano, the winner of the Palio, the ever handsome hero, was wrapped entirely in silver, his silk stomacher embroidered with pearls and silver, a giant ruby in his cap; while his brother Lorenzo, perhaps not handsome but certainly an overwhelming presence, wore light armor over simple clothes. But Lorenzo carried his shield, which contained "Il Libro," the huge Medici diamond reputed to be worth 2,500 ducats.

Leonardo could see Sandro behind Giuliano, and he shouted his name; but Leonardo's voice was lost in the din of twenty thousand other voices. He looked for Niccolò, but he could not see him with Sandro or the Medici. He pushed his way forward, but he had to pass through an army of the feared Medici-supported Companions of the Night, the darkly-dressed Dominican friars who held the informal but hated title of *inquisitore*. And they were backed up by Medici sympathizers sumptuously outfitted by Lorenzo in armor and livery of red velvet and gold.

Finally, one of the guards recognized him, and he escorted Leonardo through the sweaty, nervous troops toward Lorenzo and his entourage by the edge of the garden.

But Leonardo was not to reach them.

The air seemed heavy and fouled, as if the crowd's perspiration was rising like heat, distorting shape and perspective. Then the crowds became quiet, as Lorenzo addressed them and pointed to the sky.

Everyone looked heavenward.

And like some gauzy fantastical winged creature that Dante might have contemplated for his *Paradisio*, the Great Bird soared over Florence, circling high above the church and gardens, riding the updrafts and the currents that swirled invisibly above the towers and domes and spires of the city. Leonardo caught his breath, for the pilot certainly looked like Niccolò; surely a boy rather than a full-bodied man. He looked like an awkward angel with translucent gauze wings held in place with struts of wood and cords of twine. Indeed, the glider was as white as heaven, and Niccolò—if it was Niccolò—was dressed in a sheer white robe.

The boy sailed over the Pazzi troops like a bird swooping above a chimney, and seasoned soldiers fell to the ground in fright, or awe, and prayed; only Jacopo Pazzi, his sons, and the Archbishop remained steady on their horses. As did, of course, Lorenzo and his retinue.

And Leonardo could hear a kind of buzzing, as if he were in the midst of an army of cicadas, as twenty thousand citizens prayed to the soaring angel for their lives as they clutched and clicked black rosaries.

The heavens had opened to give them a sign, just as they had for the Hebrews at Sinai.

The boy made a tight circle around the gardens and dropped a single fragile shell that exploded on impact, throwing off great streams of fire and shards of shrapnel that cut down and burned trees and grass and shrub. Then he dropped another, which was off mark, and dangerously close to Lorenzo's entourage. A group of people were cut down by the shrapnel, and lay choking and bleeding in the streets. Fire danced across the piazza. Horses stampeded. Soldiers and citizens alike ran in panic. The Medici and Pazzi distanced themselves from the garden, their frightened troops closing around them like Roman phalanxes. Leonardo would certainly not be able to get close to the First Citizen now. He shouted at Niccolò in anger and frustration, for surely these people would die; and Leonardo would be their murderer. He had just killed them with his dreams and drawings. Here was truth. Here was revelation. He had murdered these unfortunate strangers as surely as he had killed Tista. It was as if his invention now had a life of its own, independent of its creator.

As the terrified mob raged around him, Leonardo found refuge in an alcove between two buildings and watched his Great Bird soar in great circles over the city. The sun was setting, and the high, thin cirrus clouds were stained deep red and purple. Leonardo prayed that Niccolò would have sense enough to fly westward, away from the city, where he could hope to land safely on open ground; but the boy was showing off and underestimated the capriciousness of the winds. He suddenly fell, as if dropped, toward the brick and stone below him. He shifted weight and swung his hips, trying desperately to recover. An updraft picked him up like a dust devil, and he soared skyward on heavenly breaths of warm air.

God's grace.

He seemed to be more cautious now, for he flew toward safer grounds to the west...but then he suddenly descended, falling, dropping behind the backshadowed buildings; and Leonardo could well imagine that the warm updraft that had lifted Niccolò had popped like a water bubble.

So did the boy fall through cool air, probably to his death.

Leonardo waited a beat, watching and waiting for the Great Bird to reappear. His heart was itself like a bird beating violently in his throat. Niccolò... Prayers of supplication formed in his mind, as if of their own volition, as if Leonardo's thoughts were not his own, but belonged to some peasant from Vinci grasping at a rosary for truth and hope and redemption.

Those crowded around Leonardo could not guess that the angel had fallen...just that he had descended from the Empyrean heights to the man-made spires of Florence where the sun was blazing rainbows as it set; and Lorenzo emerged triumphantly. He stood alone on a porch so he could be seen by all and distracted the crowds with a haranguing speech that was certainly directed to the Archbishop.

Florence is invincible.

The greatest and most perfect city in the world.

Florence would conquer all its enemies.

As Lorenzo spoke, Leonardo saw, as if in a lucid dream, dark skies filled with his flying machines. He saw his hempen bombs falling through the air, setting the world below on fire. Indeed, with these machines Lorenzo could conquer the Papal States and Rome itself; could burn the Pope out of the Vatican and become more powerful than any of the Caesars.

An instant later Leonardo was running, navigating the maze of alleys and streets to reach Niccolò. Niccolò was all that mattered. If the boy was dead, certainly Lorenzo would not care. But Sandro...surely Sandro...

There was no time to worry about Sandro's loyalties.

The crowds thinned, and only once was Leonardo waylaid by street arabs who blocked his way. But when they saw that Leonardo was armed and wild and ready to draw blood, they let him pass; and he ran, blade in hand, as if he were being chased by wild beasts.

Empty streets, empty buildings, the distant thunder of the crowds constant as the roaring of the sea. All of Florence was behind Leonardo, who searched for Niccolò in what might have been ancient ruins but for the myriad telltale signs that life still flowed all about here, and soon would again. Alleyways became shadows, and there was a blue tinge to the air. Soon it would be dark. A few windows already glowed tallow yellow in the balconied apartments above him.

He would not easily find Niccolò here. The boy could have fallen anywhere; and in grief and desperation, Leonardo shouted his name. His voice echoed against the high building walls; someone answered in falsetto *voce*, followed by laughter. But then Leonardo heard horses galloping through the streets, heard men's voices calling to each other. Lorenzo's men? Pazzi? There was a shout, and Leonardo knew they had found what they were looking for. Frantic, he hurried toward the soldiers, but what would he do when he found Niccolò wrapped in the wreckage of the Great Bird? Tell a dying boy that he, Leonardo, couldn't fly his own invention because he was afraid?

I was trying to make it safe, Niccolò.

He found Lorenzo's Companions of the Night in a piazza surrounded by tenements. They carried torches, and at least twenty of the well-armed priests were on horseback. Their horses were fitted out in black, as if both horses and riders had come directly from Hell; one of the horses pulled a cart covered with canvass.

Leonardo could see torn fustian and taffeta and part of the Great Bird's rudder section hanging over the red and blue striped awning of a balcony. And there, on the ground below was the upper wing assembly, intact. Other bits of cloth slid along the ground like foolscap.

Several *inquisitore* huddled over an unconscious figure.

Niccolò.

Beside himself with grief, Leonardo rushed headlong into the piazza; but before he could get halfway across the court, he was intercepted by a dozen Dominican soldiers. "I am Leonardo da Vinci," he shouted, but that seemed to mean nothing to them. These young Wolves of the Church were ready to hack him to pieces for the sheer pleasure of feeling the heft of their swords.

"Do not harm him," shouted a familiar voice.

Sandro Botticelli.

He was dressed in the thick, black garb of the *inquisitore*. "What are you doing here, Leonardo? You're a bit late." Anger and sarcasm was evident in his voice.

But Leonardo was concerned only with Niccolò, for two brawny *inquisitore* were lifting him into the cart. He pushed past Sandro and mindless of consequences pulled one of the soldiers out of the way to see the boy. Leonardo winced as he looked at the boy's smashed skull and bruised body—arms and legs broken, extended at wrong angles—and turned away in relief.

This was not Niccolò; he had never seen this boy before.

"Niccolò is with Lorenzo," Sandro said, standing beside Leonardo. "Lorenzo considered allowing Niccolò to fly your machine, for the boy knows almost as much about it as you."

"Has he flown the Great Bird?"

After a pause, Sandro said, "Yes...but against

Lorenzo's wishes. That's probably what saved his life." Sandro gazed at the boy in the cart, who was now covered with the torn wings of the Great Bird, which, in turn, was covered with canvass. "When Lorenzo discovered what Niccolò had done, he would not allow him near any of your flying machines, except to help train this boy, Giorgio, who was in his service. A nice boy, may God take his soul."

"Then Niccolò is safe?" Leonardo asked.

"Yes, the holy fathers are watching over him."

"You mean these cutthroats?"

"Watch how you speak, Leonardo. Lorenzo kept Niccolò safe for you, out of love for you. And how have you repaid him...by being a traitor?"

"Don't ever say that to me, even in jest."

"I'm not jesting, Leonardo. You've failed Lorenzo... and your country, failed them out of fear. Even a child such as Niccolò could see that."

"Is that what you think?"

Sandro didn't reply.

"Is that what Niccolò told you?"

"Yes."

Leonardo would not argue, for the stab of truth unnerved him, even now. "And you, why are you here?"

"Because Lorenzo trusts me. As far as Florence and the Archbishop is concerned, the angel flew and caused fire to rain from Heaven. And is in Heaven now as we speak." He shrugged and nodded to the *inquisitore*, who mounted their horses.

"So now you command the Companions of the Night

instead of the divine power of the painter," Leonardo said, the bitterness evident in his voice. "Perhaps we are on different sides now, Little Bottle."

"*I'm* on the side of Florence," Sandro said. "And against her enemies. *You* care only for your inventions."

"And my friends," Leonardo said quietly, pointedly.

"Perhaps for Niccolò, perhaps a little for me; but more for yourself."

"How many of my flying machines does Lorenzo have now?" Leonardo asked, but Sandro turned away from him and rode behind the cart that carried the corpse of the angel and the broken bits of the Great Bird. Once again, Leonardo felt the numbing, rubbery sensation of great fatigue, as if he had turned into an old man, as if all his work, now finished, had come to nothing. He wished only to be rid of it all: his inventions, his pain and guilt. He could not bear even to be in Florence, the place he loved above all others.

There was no place for him now.

* * * * * * *

Leonardo could be seen as a shadow moving inside his canvass-covered makeshift workshop, which was brightly lit by several water lamps and a small fire. Other shadows passed across the vellum-covered windows of the surrounding buildings like mirages in the Florentine night. Much of the city was dark, for few could afford tallow and oil.

But Leonardo's tented workshop was brighter than

most, for he was methodically burning his notes and papers, his diagrams and sketches of his new soaring machine. After the notebooks were curling ash and smoke rising through a single vent in the canvass, he burned his box-shaped models of wood and cloth: kites and flying machines of various design; and then, at the last, he smashed his partially completed soaring machine...smashed the spars and rudder, smashed the box-like wings, tore away the webbing and fustian, which burned like hemp in the crackling fire.

As if Leonardo could burn his ideas from his thoughts.

Yet he could not help but feel that the rising smoke was the very stuff of his ideas and invention. And he was spreading them for all to inhale like poisonous phantasms.

Lorenzo already had Leonardo's flying machines.

More children would die...

He burned his drawings and paintings, his portraits and madonnas and varnished visions of fear, then left the makeshift studio like a sleepwalker heading back to his bed; and the glue and fustian and broken spars ignited, glowing like coals, then burst, exploded, shot like fireworks or silent hempen bombs until the canvass was ablaze. Leonardo was far away by then and couldn't hear the shouts of Andrea and Francesco and the apprentices as they rushed to put out the fire.

* * * * * * *

Niccolò found Leonardo standing upon the same mountain where Tista had fallen to his death. His face and shirt streaked with soot and ash, Leonardo stared down into the misty valley below. There was the Palazzo Vecchio, and the dome of the Duomo reflecting the early morning sun...and beyond, created out of the white dressing of the mist itself, was his memory cathedral. Leonardo gazed at it...into it. He relived once again Tista's flight into death and saw the paintings he had burned; indeed, he looked into Hell, into the future where he glimpsed the dark skies filled with Lorenzo's soaring machines, raining death from the skies, the winged devices that Leonardo would no longer claim as his own. He wished he had never dreamed of the Great Bird. But now it was too late for anything but regret.

What was done could not be undone.

"Maestro!" Niccolò shouted, pulling Leonardo away from the cliff edge, as if he, Leonardo, had been about to launch himself without wings or harness into the fog. As perhaps he was.

"Everyone has been frantic with worry for you," Niccolò said, as if he was out of breath.

"I should not think I would have been missed."

Niccolò snorted, which reminded Leonardo that he was still a child, no matter how grown up he behaved and had come to look. "You nearly set Maestro Verrocchio's bottega on fire."

"Surely my lamps would extinguish themselves when out of oil, and the fire was properly vented. I myself—"

"Neighbors saved the bottega," Niccolò said, as if impatient to get on to other subjects. "They alerted *everyone.*"

"Then there was no damage?" Leonardo asked.

"Just black marks on the walls."

"Good," Leonardo said, and he walked away from Niccolò, who followed after him. Ahead was a thick bank of mist the color of ash, a wall that might have been a sheer drop, but behind which in reality were fields and trees.

"I knew I would find you here," Niccolò said.

"And how did you know that, Nicco?"

The boy shrugged.

"You must go back to the bottega," Leonardo said.

"I'll go back with you, Maestro."

"I'm not going back." The morning mist was all around them; it seemed to be boiling up from the very ground. There would be rain today and heavy skies.

"Where are you going?"

Leonardo shrugged.

"But you've left everything behind." After a beat, Niccolò said, "I'm going with you."

"No, young ser."

"But what will I do?"

Leonardo smiled. "I would guess that you'll stay with Maestro Verrochio until Lorenzo invites you to be his guest. But you must promise me you'll never fly any of his machines."

Niccolò promised; of course, Leonardo knew that

the boy would do as he wished. "I did not believe you were afraid, Maestro."

"Of course not, Nicco."

"I shall walk with you a little way."

"No."

Leonardo left Niccolò behind, as if he could leave the past for a new, innocent future. As if he had never invented bombs and machines that could fly. As if, but for his paintings, he had never existed at all.

Niccolò called to him...then his voice faded away, and was gone.

Soon the rain stopped and the fog lifted, and Leonardo looked up at the red tinged sky.

Perhaps in hope.

Perhaps in fear.

ABOUT THE AUTHOR

JACK DANN is a multiple-award winning author who has written or edited over seventy-five books, including the ground-breaking novels *The Man Who Melted*, *The Memory Cathedral*—which is an international bestseller, the Civil War novel *The Silent*, which *Library Journal* called "narrative storytelling at its best...most emphatically recommended," and *Bad Medicine*, which has been compared to the works of Jack Kerouac and Hunter S. Thompson. His counterfactual biography *The Rebel: an Imagined Life of James Dean* has been called "a love letter to the 60's" and "a significant and very gripping novel." A companion James Dean short story collection entitled *Promised Land* has also been published in Great Britain, as has Dann's most recent short novel *The Economy of Light*. His short fiction can be found in collections such as *Timetipping*, *Jubilee*, *Visitations*, and *The Fiction Factory*. His latest anthologies are *Dreaming Again*, *The Dragon Book* (with Gardner Dozois), and *Australian Legends* (with Jonathan Strahan).

Dann is a recipient of the Nebula Award, the Australian Aurealis Award (twice), the Ditmar Award (four times), the World Fantasy Award, the Peter McNamara Achievement Award, the Peter McNamara Convenors Award for Excellence, and the Premios Gilgamés de Narrativa Fantástica award. He has also been honored by the Mark Twain Society (Esteemed Knight). Dann lives in Australia on a farm overlooking the sea and "commutes" back and forth to Los Angeles and New York. He is married to the writer Janeen Webb. His website is:

www.jackdann.com

THE DIAMOND PIT

Winner of the Australian Ditmar Award and short-listed for the Hugo, Nebula, Locus, and Aurelis Awards, *The Diamond Pit* is a celebration of larger-than-life America and the American dream. It's about William Randolph Hearst and Horatio Alger, it's about the very, *very* nouveau-riche, and it's also a brilliant homage to F. Scott Fitzgerald's dreamy adventure story, "The Diamond as Big as the Ritz."

The magazine *Ideomancer* called it an action story, a moral meditation, and a critique of pulp heroes that takes place "against the backdrop of early airplanes, kidnappings, ragtime piano, spectacular châteaux, Faulknerian histories, elaborate gardens, romantic interludes, catacombs, battles, infidelity, and cold-blooded murder."

Borgo Press Books by JACK DANN

Da Vinci Rising
The Diamond Pit: A Science Fiction Novel
The Economy of Light
Jubilee

THE DIAMOND PIT

A SCIENCE FICTION NOVEL

JACK DANN

THE BORGO PRESS

MMX

THE DIAMOND PIT

Copyright © 2001, 2010 by Jack Dann

FIRST EDITION

Published by Wildside Press LLC

www.wildsidebooks.com

DEDICATION

Both of these books are for my lovely pal,

Caren Bohrman

CONTENTS

Chapter One 9

Chapter Two 15

Chapter Three 27

Chapter Four 39

Chapter Five 51

Chapter Six 65

Chapter Seven 69

Chapter Eight 81

Chapter Nine 93

Chapter Ten 107

Chapter Eleven 125

About the Author 127

CHAPTER ONE

Homage to F. Scott...

I'd be flyin' to find!
My Miss One-of-a-kind!
If I could only get—
If only I could get—
out'a this jail!...

—"Rumplemayer's
Basement Blues," 1921

It was like being in a storm, except I heard the thunder first. That was the sound of a dozen anti-aircraft guns firing at us from the summit of a sheer butte that rose like a monolith above the cruel curls of the Montana Rockies.

The setting sun was wreathed with gauzy clouds, and it tinted the cliffs and crevasses below as pink as stained glass flamingos. We were flying a British Moth with a 60-hp de Havilland motor—those Brits could certainly make an airplane. The Moth was steady as a table and was Joel's and my favorite for wing walking

and stepping off from one plane onto another. I was in the front cockpit this time, just along for the ride. It had been Joel's idea to borrow the boss's beaut and skip out after our last performance to investigate "something goofy" in the mountains near Hades, which was more bare rock than a village set in the saddle between a mountain that looked like a two-knuckled fist and the mountain that was shooting bullets at us.

Joel swore and shouted though the communication tube and tried to get us the hell out of there, as bullets tore into the fuselage. Another burst hit the upper wing just above my head, which was where the fuel tank was located. My face was spattered with gasoline and I figured then and there that I had just bought the farm; Joel was shouting through the tube to tell me that everything was okay—when we were hit again.

I heard a ping as a bullet hit the motor, and an instant later I could barely see through the oily smoke and fire. I gagged on the burnt exhalations of fuel and oil that smeared over my goggles as the Moth went into a dive. Reflexively, I took over the controls, which were linked to the front cockpit, God bless Mr. Geoffrey de Havilland. I shouted back at Joel through the tube and pulled as hard as I could on the stick while working the rudder and aileron pedals. The compass was going all wacky, as though someone was playing over it with a magnet, pulling the needle this way and that. Although I couldn't see Joel, I *knew* that he had been hit. Another wave of heat swept over me and I figured I'd be lucky to have another few seconds before the fuel tank blew

Joel and me right out of the postcard pink and purple sky.

I'd always wondered what I'd be thinking about in my last moments. I'd wondered about it every time I climbed into a Spad during Bloody April of 1917; I could fly as well as most anybody, although I was no Rickenbacker. I had figured I was going to get it in '17 or '18, but I never even took a bullet, not a scratch—I had the proverbial angel on my wing—and now here I was, about to get it in 1923, which was *supposed* to be the best year of my life. I remembered Dr. Coué's prayer, which everyone was saying: "Day by day in every way I am getting better and better."

Better and better.

"Joel," I shouted through the tube, "you're going to be okay. We're going to be okay." *Day by day in every fucking way*, and I felt that hot, sweaty tightness all over my face like I always do when I'm going to cry, but I slipped out of that because the old girl was making a whining keening sort of a noise, and then the motor sputtered and everything became summer afternoon quiet, except for the snapping of the wing wires...

And I found myself counting, counting slowly and the ground spun through the smoke, and I kept the nose up as the valley floor rose like an elevator the size of Manhattan, and I wasn't thinking about anything, not about dying or the tank exploding or the smoke or the smell of the oil...or my Mother, or Lisa, whom I had only dated twice, but she had gone down on the first date and

said she loved me, and she had so many freckles, and three curly black hairs between her breasts, I remembered those three black hairs as I counted and by one-hundred-and-forty-seven I expected the giant hand of God to slap me right into the canyon floor and the fuel tank to explode like the sun and—

* * * * * * *

IT WAS DARK when they found me, but the moon was so big and bloated that everything looked like it was coated with silvery dust, except the shadows, where the moon dust couldn't settle. I don't know whether they woke me or whether it was the drip from the fuel tank, but once I realized I was alive and that this was certainly not heaven, I felt most every part of my body begin to ache. I moved my legs to make sure I still had them, and I tried to swat at the Negroes who were pulling me out of the cockpit. I don't know what was in my head because they were big men, and I was just swatting away, but they didn't throw me about or mistreat me or ask me any questions; it was as if they were just handling a fragile piece of merchandise, nothing that was alive, just merchandise. I started coughing as soon as they moved me, and I craned my neck for one last look at the plane...and at Joel, the poor dumb jake who just had to see if the stories were true about a grand castle on the mountain. Now Joel was dead, his face shot off, and I was being carried away by giants who were speaking a dialect like none I'd ever heard; in fact, I couldn't understand a word, although

I couldn't help but think it was *some* form of Southern English.

And we hadn't even seen a castle.

Damn you, Joel.

I blacked out, and woke up as I was being thrown this way and that in the seat of some kind of souped-up, armored suburban; but this beast hadn't rolled off any of Henry Ford's production lines. It was a chimerical combination of tank and automobile. Instead of windows, the passenger cab had thick glass portholes, and Lewis machine guns were mounted on the hood and trunk. I could hardly hear the motor as we sped and jostled into the long purple shadows of the mountains above, and my captors were as quiet as the mountains.

When I woke again, after dreaming that Joel was fine and we were back in the Moth gliding silently through the night over castles and fairy lights, I found myself in the air indeed. The suburban was being hoisted up the sheer face of a cliff, rising into the milky moonlight; and, startled, I bolted forward. The two black giants beside me pulled me back into the cushioned softness of the seat and held me there. I tried to talk to them, to ask them what was going on, but they just shook their heads as though they couldn't understand me.

Then with a bounce the suburban was lowered onto solid ground. Two men and a boy were waiting beside a crane used on aircraft carriers to hoist boats and planes; and as they removed the cables that had been attached to the hub-guards of the huge truck-tired wheels,

they spoke to each other in that peculiar dialect that was both familiar...and unfamiliar.

Once again we drove, only now we were that much closer to the sky. As I looked out through the porthole on my right, the moon looked green, radiating its wan, sickly light through filigrees of cloud; and the road made of tapestry brick was as straight and neat and ghostly as the fog and mist that clung to it.

We passed a lake that could have been a dark mirror misted with breath and reflecting the stars and bloated moon. I caught a sudden scent of pine, and then I saw it, a chateau—no, rather a moon-painted castle—with opalescent terraces, walkways, mosque-like towers, and outbuildings rising from broad, tree-lined lawns.

But my destination, alas, would be otherwise.

CHAPTER TWO

"Hell's bells, it's almost noon."

"Clarence, how would you know whether it was noon or what? Your wristwatch has stopped so many times, it could be midnight."

"Don't call me Clarence or I'll break your legs."

"You an' whose army?"

I snapped awake and looked around the room, which resolved around me. Walls, floor, ceiling seemed to be made of a piece, a smooth, translucent layer of opal, which glowed with light; but I could not discern the source of the suffusing light, nor could I see the inset marks of tile, only high, straight, iridescent planes that reached to a ceiling of the same substance. I was lying in a comfortable feather bed with a jewel-inlaid footboard; the bed and an ebony table and elbow chair were the only pieces of furniture in this smooth, glittering travesty of a monk's cell.

"Well, sleeping beauty has awoke," said Clarence. He had a pale, freckled complexion, red hair that was graying, and a pop-eyed look, no doubt because his eyebrows were so white that they seemed to disappear.

"You're probably still feelin' dopey," he said to me. "The slaves drugged you so Old Jefferson could do his interrogation. Takes a while for it to wear off."

"Well, they didn't drug *me*," said the man who had been goading Clarence about his name. He was bald, tall, and aggressive; and he had a ruddy complexion like Clarence—it was as if both men were of the same Irish and Dutch ancestry. Both wore pants and shirts that looked like pajamas, except Clarence wore an aviator's jacket and the bald man wore a cap.

Eleven other men were standing in the room behind them, and a short wiry aviator—I was sure right then and there that they were *all* aviators—said, "Old man Jefferson drugged *everybody*. Even you, Monty. You just don't remember none of it, while we do."

"But none of us remembers much," said Clarence, who introduced himself as Skip, and then introduced me to Monty Kleeck and Farley James and Rick Moss and Carl Crocker and Eddie Barthelmet, Harry Talmadge, Keith Boardman, Gregory "Cissy" Schneck, "Snap" Samuel Geraldson, and Stephen Freeburg, who "was the only Jew in this mess of Protestants."

"You a Jew too?" asked the skinny, nervous upchuck who was called Cissy. There was a meanness in his voice, but he wasn't big enough to back it up, and I knew he was more dangerous than the three-hundred-pound hulk they called Snap.

I thought about saying yes, but I figured I might be here a while—maybe for life, from the look of them—and so I said, "No, I'm Catholic. You have a problem

with that?"

"No, no," said Cissy, backing off. "I got no problem with Christians." Then in an undertone he said, "Long as they're Christians..."

"Where the hell am I?" I asked, some of the muzziness from the drugs finally clearing—if, indeed, I'd been drugged. I directed myself to Stephen Freeburg, who had the same kind of dark, sharp features as Rudolph Valentino, who last I heard had gone to prison for bigamy.

"You're in the Randolph Estes Jefferson Hotel," Freeburg said, smiling. "It's probably the fanciest, most comfortable jail in the world. And unless you can think of something we haven't, you're here for life."

"No, we'll get out," said Carl Crocker, a short, overweight, squarish chap with bristly brown hair— they must feed these guys pretty well, I thought; but everything was just words and thoughts wriggling like worms in sand. Nothing seemed real. My mouth felt like it was stuffed with wire. My eyes were burning. My head was pounding. Wake up, I told myself. Wake the hell up.

"Yeah, your tunnel," Freeburg said sarcastically. "Next, you and Snap will be drilling straight down." Everyone laughed at that.

I guess I looked bemused because Eddie Barthelmet, a reedy yet muscular man with thinning black hair, whom I figured immediately as the sort who kept his own counsel, said, "It's solid diamond underneath us. Hardest substance in the world."

I shook my head and grinned. I could take being the butt of the joke.

"I'm not joshing you. The whole goddamn mountain is diamond, except for the rock and stone above. And it's all owned by the Old Man, who isn't too willing to share, which is why we're down here, and he's up there." Everyone laughed at that, and Eddie just nodded toward the ceiling, as if some omniscient being were standing right above us. Then after a pause, he asked, "Did you happen to notice if your compass seemed to go wild when you approached the mountain?"

"Yeah," I said. "But I figured it had been knocked out of whack."

"No, the same thing happened to me. None of the others remember anything being wrong with their compasses, so I figure that the Old Man concocted something new. An artificial magnetic field, or something like that."

"Well, if he could change the official maps of the United States, he could screw up our compasses, I suppose," Clarence said. I didn't figure him to be the brightest of the bunch, but I couldn't help but like him. He seemed genuinely concerned, and maybe it was the way he slouched or patted the chair, I don't know, but for some reason I had the feeling that he was really at home here. He turned to me and said, "Don't worry, you'll be meeting the Old Man soon enough. And when you're ready, I'll give you the tour of the place and help you get set up. Now you think you're ready to tell us your name and how you came to be flyin' out

here? You *were* flyin'...?"

I nodded and told them my name—Paul Orsatti—
and I told them that I was a mail pilot, which I'd been
for a while, until I got myself fired from New York
Chicago Air Transport for being self-righteous; and I
wasn't going to tell them that I'd been kicking around
for the past year as a roustabout stunt flier, working for
crummy outfits like Pitkin's Circle-Q Flying Circus.
Or that I'd been playing piano in cheapjack speakeasies
for nothing more than drinks and whatever change the
Doras and ossified lounge lizards could spare. I didn't
tell them about Joel, and how he'd heard rumors about
there being something strange in the mountain near
Hades. I only told them I'd gotten a bit off-course—
next thing I knew I was being shot at.

And as if I'd been caught telling a lie by the Lord God
Almighty Himself, I heard a voice calling everyone to
attention.

A broadcast from above:

"Well, boys," said God. "Don't you want to have a
chat? My daughter's accompanying me, so y'all better
be on your best behavior, gentlemen. None of your
usual filthy street patois. Now shake a leg!"

Everyone started swearing and complaining, but
they obediently moved out of my room toward where
the voice was probably coming from, and Skip pulled
me along, telling me that I might as well know my
keeper and get it in my head that I'm here and that's
that and how it's not so bad, in fact, probably better
than we'd ever have it back home in the *real* world.

We walked through a seamless corridor made of the same stuff as the walls, floor, and ceiling of the room where I'd awakened. Dim, pervasive light radiated wanly from the ceiling, and doorways were evenly spaced on both sides. I caught glimpses into other rooms, some larger than others, some dark, some brightly lit, and could see rooms that led into other corridors. I was in a polished, many-hued glass warren that could hold many more men than we who were here now. We crowded into an empty room, which was a high tower...a terminus of sorts.

I looked up at a large, brightly lit opening covered with grating and saw a man looking down at us—I assumed he was Mr. Randolph Estes Jefferson.

Some sort of lens must have also covered the opening because Mr. Jefferson seemed greatly magnified and also slightly distorted, as though his girth was being pulled toward the edges of the opening. He looked to be about forty-five and had one of those faces that always remind me of a pug dog: jowly and fleshy, yet absolutely intent—the proverbial dog with a bone. He stood erect, as though he was wearing military gear instead of a straw boater, blue blazer, and white flannel Oxford bags. If it weren't for that face and his bearing, he could have been a fashion plate. He was swinging what I thought was a cane, swinging it back and forth over the opening to the tower of our prison (but which was, in effect, just a grating in the grass from his perspective). A girl of perhaps eighteen stood beside her pug dog father. She wore a thin blue blouse with a

pleated tennis skirt and a blue bandeau to keep her hair in place. Her hair was blond, curly, and bobbed, and although I couldn't see the color of her eyes, I imagined they would be blue. Her mouth was crimson, her face tan against the blue bandeau. Even with the slight distortion, I could see that she was perfection—a pure vision of youth and freshness and beauty.

"Hey, leave the old guy and come on down here."

"Push him through the grate, we'll take care of everything for you."

"They don't call me snugglepup for nottin'," Crocker shouted, and most everyone was laughing...except Mr. Jefferson. His daughter smiled warmly at all of us and bowed, as though she was being presented at a cotillion in New York or Chicago or Paris.

"Gentlemen," said Mr. Jefferson, "remember your manners. If y'all continue to embarrass me before my daughter, I shall be happy to instruct my slaves to forget to supply you with your daily rations, which I presume are to your expectations?"

"Slaves?" I asked Skip, who was standing beside me and rubbernecking, to get a better look at the girl.

"Yeah," Skip said, "he's got hundreds of 'em, I guess."

"The rations are fine, except we could do without the fish eggs," said Rick Moss, a short unshaven man, who was so muscular that he looked like he might have been a weight lifter.

"So the rations of caviar are not appreciated," Jefferson said. "Well, we'll take that item off the menu."

Randolph Estes Jefferson sounded cheerful, as if he were merely a waiter taking an order and listening to customers' complaints. "Now my Phoebe loves caviar," he said, putting his arm around his daughter, "so I, of course, just assumed y'all would too. I figured your generation with all your jazz and Wall Street savvy was more sophisticated than mine."

But Harry Talmadge and Keith Boardman, who were standing beside me and looking quietly bored, were not exactly what you'd call jazz babies—Harry looked to be in his middle forties, but it would be difficult to guess whether Keith was in his fifties or sixties. He looked well fed and well exercised, as though he were someone who could afford to pamper himself and maintain his youth.

I thought it odd that our jailer Mr. Jefferson used "y'all" like someone from the Deep South, yet he had no accent at all...which was probably the same thing as having a Midwest accent.

"Well, *I* don't mind the caviar," said fat Snap Geraldson. "I guess that makes me the only sophisticated guy down here." That got a laugh.

"Are you here to bait us like bears, or have you come up with a solution to our problem?" asked Freeburg.

"Ah, Mr. Freeburg, you are always so angry and so ready to argue how many angels might rest on the head of a pin. Aren't you satisfied with the Talmud I provided for your studies?"

"I've simply taken the bait," Freeburg said.

"Well, good for you, then. But we've been over and

over my predicament. I—being a man of conscience—must bear the burden of keeping y'all in prison because to free you would be harmful to my family and myself and my retainers. You'll soon come to understand that, too, Mr. Orsatti."

I almost took a step back when he addressed me.

"I trust you're getting settled in comfortably," he continued. "The other boys will show you the ropes. If anyone mistreats you, just slip a note into the food slot. It'll reach me in due course. I've developed quite a paternalistic affection for all of you. Quite."

"We'd promise not to peach on you," cried Carl Crocker. "And that's the honest truth. Just let us go. Give us a chance."

"Ah, but you couldn't help yourself, could you, Mr. Crocker," Jefferson said, as he pulled a lawn chair over for Phoebe and then disappeared for a few seconds to return with a chair for himself. "You'd have to tell *some*one. And if you could come back and get past my slaves and my guns, why then *you'd* be the richest man on Earth. Would you like me to send some more gems down to you? You can have whatever you wish—diamonds, rubies, sapphires, a birthstone of your own weight."

"Won't do me any good down here," Carl said.

"Ah, you see, value is relative. But once you got away from here, these diamonds and rubies and sapphires would be worth as much as life itself. Surely you can see that?"

"No, I can't," said Carl.

"As I've asked you before, do you want me to have your wives and girlfriends brought here? I'll extend your accommodations. Y'all would have everything you could wish for."

"Except freedom," said Eddie Barthelmet. "What would it take to buy that?"

"You can't *buy* anything from me," said Mr. Jefferson. "All that I give is as a gift. When last we spoke—how long ago was that? Perhaps a few months ago?—I asked if you could come up with a better solution. Well, this is your chance. Propose."

"So you can dispose," said Eddie.

"Very good, very good indeed. The newer members seem to be quicker than the rest of you. You'll need to study to keep up."

"Then let us have some newspapers," shouted Crocker.

"Yeah, is prohibition repealed yet?"

"What would you care?" Mr. Jefferson said. "Whatever spirits you request are sent to you. What more could you ask for?"

That elicited shouting and swearing, and Mr. Jefferson just smiled and held up his hands. "Well, gentlemen, I see that we're finished."

"We do care about whether prohibition has been repealed," Eddie shouted up to Mr. Jefferson. "Just as we care about what the stock market is doing, what's the new dance, what's happening with the Fascists in Italy, what's the latest Zane Grey, is Dempsey still heavyweight champion, who won the World Series?"

"Giants over the Yankees, 5-3 in the fifth," I said in a low voice. Eddie nodded to me, and a few of the other boys started to argue the merits of the Giants and the Yankees.

"There's your answer," Mr. Jefferson said. He could only have heard me if he had listening devices planted in here, which, of course, he would.

"We need access to newspapers...and the radio," Eddie said.

"It will only stir you up, son, and make you yearn for what you can't have," Jefferson said. "You've got a library of the great classics of literature. That should be edification enough."

"I want *The Saturday Evening Post*," Crocker said.

"I want *The Strand*."

"I want Phoebe."

"Good-bye, gentlemen," Jefferson said.

"Wait," shouted Eddie. "Why not at least give us leave? At least, let one or two of us out for a few days. You could have your slaves guard us to make sure we couldn't run for it. We could at least see a ball game, or a movie. Then you could bring us back, and take another group out. As you are always fond of telling us, 'Money's no object.'"

Jefferson made a clucking noise and said, "That's a new twist, Mr. Barthelmet. Very good, indeed. Except my slaves would have to gag you and bind you so you wouldn't shout for help or make a run for it, and the constabulary might look askance at that. But even if you were a model parolee, you'd come back and yearn

for what you'd seen. No, it would just deepen the pain of your circumstances. Allow me to bring your wives or lovers or friends to you."

"No," shouted Rick Moss, and he was echoed by the others.

"It's bad enough you've buried us."

"Let us the hell out of here, you bastid."

"Well, gentlemen, I think that's more than enough," Jefferson said. "Come on, Phoebe, enough diversion for you." He stood up, and I could see then that he had been holding a golf club, not a cane. We were buried under his golf course, and he and his daughter were just out playing eighteen holes. The sonovabitch!

There was a grating noise, and the opening above went black.

"Wait," I shouted reflexively.

The ceiling irised open, and Jefferson and his beautiful Phoebe looked down at us. "Yes, Mr. Orsatti?" he asked.

"I'd like a piano."

Jefferson laughed and said, "Done."

"That's all we need, more noise—"

"We could use some of that—"

"You boys can dance with each other—"

"It beats what we're doin' now—"

But before the ceiling closed, I could see Phoebe looking down—right at *me*—and smiling.

CHAPTER THREE

The piano arrived, as promised. It was a special-edition, pearl-white Steinway grand, which produced a huge, full orchestral sound, yet the keys had such an incredibly fast action that I couldn't help but open up with a boogie-woogie medley. My feet stomped on the floor as my left hand flew over the keys beating out syncopated rhythms that were so tricky that I dared not watch what I was doing, lest I falter; and my right hand, weaving various melodies through the rhythms of my left, might as well have had a mind of its own.

I was a one-man band.

I was also, needless to say, half in the proverbial bag. But so was everyone else, except Cissy Schneck and Farley James, a nice British fellow who had been an Oxford don before the war. I found out from Skip that he had been an ace pilot. He'd come over here to compete in the ocean-to-ocean air race in '19, the same year the Cincinnati Reds beat the Sox in the eighth game, which was a miracle. So was Farley James, I guess, because he'd come in second place and decided to stay and start an air flying company with Charlie Lindbergh. That surprised the hell out of me because

Joel, may God rest his soul, said he'd worked for Lindbergh for a while.

"Hey, Farley," I called, and he dutifully came over to the piano, where Skip formally introduced us.

"Fahley, z'ish is Pauhhzzotti..."

"Skip tells me you had some business with Charlie Lindbergh."

Farley nodded, smiling at Skip who then began to lead everyone in another chorus of another new song I had played for them.

"*Do you have any bananas?*"

"*Yes! We have no bananas!*"

"Do you know Charlie?" Farley asked.

"Yeah, I met him through a friend of mine, Joel Wagner. Ring any bells?"

"Small world. Sure, I remember Joel. Good aviator. Dependable. What's he doing with himself these days?"

"He's dead."

Farley looked shocked, and he stared down at his shoes, which were so highly polished he could probably see his face in them.

"Did you ever talk to him about...a castle up in the mountains?" I asked.

His thin, sensitive face was tight as shellacked paper. He looked straight at me and said, "No." After a pause, he said, "But he was shot down with you, wasn't he..."

I started playing "Look for the Silver Lining," which everyone knew, then "Wild Rose," and "Ma—He's Making Eyes at Me" which Snap Geraldson sang in falsetto. That was something to hear...and see. Isn't

often an elephant imitates a parrot being squeezed into a juicer. I played and sang Bessie Smith's "Downhearted Blues," and, of course, nobody knew who she was; but Rick Moss and Snap started dancing with each other. I taught them how to Charleston, which had just become all the rage, and all hell broke loose with everybody swaying back and forth, slapping their knees, swiveling around on the balls of their feet, and falling over like they'd been dancing in a marathon for two weeks. After a while I started playing slower tunes again like "All by Myself" and "Who's Sorry Now," and then even a little Liszt and Bach, and the party broke up, and—

"You can't sleep on the piana."

I don't know how he did it, but somehow Skip got me up and dragged me or walked me or rolled me toward my room. I remember seeing open doors that led into rooms with pool tables and ping-pong tables. I remember a kitchen and gymnasium and a room that was so bright I could barely look into it. I passed the fabled library that God had provided with all the classics but no up-to-date *Saturday Evening Posts*, and I remember feeling a pressure around my temples; I imagined that Joel and I were back in the Moth, and the engine was on fire, and my forehead was hot, and then something squeezed my stomach, and from far away Joel or Skip or somebody said, "Hot damn," and I dreamed about beautiful Phoebe looking down at me from the perfect golf-course gardens and tennis courts of Heaven. Her eyes, set in her sun-bronzed face like

perfectly shaped transparent gems, were impossibly blue. Sky blue freedom.

And then I woke up in Skip's room.

"Drink this. Hair of the dog."

Skip probably looked worse than I did. I couldn't see him very well—my head was pulsing with pain. I guess I wasn't used to drinking real hooch. The rotgut I'd been drinking since '20 hadn't killed me, but it sure felt like the vintage Johnny Walker and Chivas Regal would.

I drank the tomato juice and brew, which Skip called "Virginia Dare." It went down like razor blades, and when I stopped being sick, I asked him why he'd decorated most every surface in the room with a towel—there was a white bath towel neatly tacked over his desk, a white dish towel on the bed table, a red face towel placed like a doily over the back of his stuffed chair, another added color and warmth to a utilitarian tallboy, and towels of various sizes and hues decorated the inside of every drawer open to my view.

"I learned how to do that when I was a kid. I spent a few years in an orphanage." He grinned. "Well, not exactly an orphanage. A private school. But same difference. After Dad popped it, and Mom decided she'd follow by sticking her head in a stove, Dad's best friend kept me in the best schools for as long as my inheritance money held out, which wasn't long."

That was more than I wanted to know about Skip's schooldays, but he seemed cheerful about it all, even about finding his mother, who he said was "blue as a

curtain." He said he'd learned about making things cozy in "the orphanage," and he'd got used to decorating with towels.

"Thanks for the bed," I said, "but you didn't have to sleep on the floor. You could've slept in my room, if you couldn't drag me that far."

"I could barely get you *this* far," Skip said. "You're heavier than you look. But I never sleep anywhere but right here. It's as much home as anything else. Some of the other guys move around. You know—"

I didn't, and I could feel the nausea working its way up to my throat.

"—sleep with each other, like that. No girls here, what else you going to do? Except get really friendly with Madam Palm and her five daughters." He grinned again, looking pop-eyed and childlike, and wagged his right hand at me. "I prefer Madam Palm."

"Can't God up there help you out with some women?"

Skip laughed and said, "Old Jefferson's very prim and proper. You heard him. The choice is wives or girlfriends, or nothin'—and he'd make you marry your girlfriend, sure as shit, not that it would matter, anyway, 'cause once they got here, they wouldn't have any choice. They'd be stuck here forever amen like we are. And who knows how dangerous it would be for them, what with all the other guys. We asked Jefferson if we could borrow some of his slave girls, although we never saw them, but he doesn't believe in whorin' and promiscuity, as he calls it, and, anyway, according to him, he wouldn't misuse his slaves."

"How does he keep slaves? It's 1923, for Chrissakes, not 1823."

Skip shrugged. "There's all kind of stories. George Bernard, who's been here the longest—over twenty years—probably knows, but he ain't saying. You didn't meet George. He's sort of a hermit, doesn't even go to the tower when the old man calls. He don't talk to no one. He wasn't no flier, that's for sure, but, like I said, he don't talk. You got to respect that, I figure. Anyway, none of us talk about the slaves since Lowell Legendre was poisoned—now he *was* a pilot, shot down just like the rest of us, only he could speak a couple of languages. He had your room, come to think of it. Anyway, he said he was learning how to talk slave-talk from one of the slaves who brung the food. That must have been some trick, 'cause I've never met any of the old man's slaves who could speak or understand one word of English. Lowell said he was getting the hang of it, though, and that once he'd figured it all out, he'd know what was going on and maybe we could figure a way out of here. But he got sick after eating dinner— it was terrible, worse than my mother—and we tried calling for someone to get us some help. But the old man and his slaves suddenly got deaf, dumb, and blind. We didn't get any food after that for a week. All we had was water. And after that, all the slaves that had anything to do with us were new. So probably best not to get too curious about them. You'll see your share."

"I want to meet this George Bernard," I said.

"I'll show you his room," Skip said, "but he won't let you in. I once—"

I made a dash for Skip's toilet, but didn't make it.

When I came around again, still hung-over with a blinding headache and a mouth that tasted like it was full of metal shavings and dirt, I was back in my room.

Old Skip must have found new reserves of strength. Or a few buddies.

* * * * * * *

George Bernard *did* receive me, as if he wasn't a prisoner like the rest of us, but a guest with special privileges. However, I waited before knocking on his door, which was a football field away from the rest of us.

I got to know my fellow inmates. I spent time in the "sun room" with Snap Geraldson discussing Edward Egan and Sam Mosberg, who took gold in the Lightweight and Light Heavyweight categories respectively at the Antwerp Olympics in '20. It was like discussing boxing with the Buddha. I played ping-pong with Carl Crocker and pool with Keith Boardman and Harry Talmadge, who wanted to be brought up to date on current events; and we argued over the Sacco and Vanzetti convictions. I swam every day in the pool, usually with Skip, who did a couple of miles a day, when he wasn't coming off a hangover, and I spent hours talking plays and movies and books with Farley James and Stephen Freeburg in the library. We discussed Conrad and Gide and Ibanez and Waley and

Apollinaire, while we drank God's good whiskey until we were ossified. And every day I practiced the piano. I played for hours, doing scales, working the life back into my fingers, which flew over the keyboard; and if I had to be here, if I was going to be trapped in this diamond pit with this ragtag group of swillers in this speakeasy prison, I'd get my hands back. I practiced the sonatas of Scarlatti and Clementi and Mozart and Bach and Schumann and Brahms, and Liszt, of course; and it all came back to me; it was like I'd never left conservatory. I played Debussy's *Études for Piano*, Ravel's *Daphnis and Chloe*, Schoenberg's *Five Piano Pieces*, which I knew by heart, and Stravinsky's *Piano-Rag Music*. I played until I was exhausted, and there were no days or nights, just melody, counterpoint, rhythm, and drinking and talking.

Was I in prison? Or purgatory?

Or Heaven, as it surely was for Skip—good food, whiskey, friends, a room tidied up with towels. But after Snap Geraldson threw a fit and hurt his back, I began to suspect that *everyone* was crazy...

That's when I decided to visit George Bernard.

* * * * * * *

"Welcome, Mr. Orsatti."

A beefy man dressed in an old-fashioned military-style smoking jacket with silk cord frogging stood hulking like a costumed bouncer in the partially closed doorway. He was the same body type as Mr. Randolph Estes Jefferson—a bull-dog endomorph—and he was

wearing flannel trousers that were so wrinkled they looked like he had been sleeping in them for weeks, which he might have been. His slippers were torn, and his sparse, curly brown hair appeared as though an electric current had passed through it only seconds before my arrival. But while the Lord God Jefferson above struck me as conceited, self-satisfied, and vital (as male members of the upper crust were trained to be), George Bernard seemed somehow incongruously tall and fat and fox-like. He sized me up, seemingly taking in every detail, and grinned.

"How do you know my name?" I asked, trying to place the ratchety noises that were emanating from all over his room. But I couldn't see past him.

Obligingly, he stepped aside.

"Skip Cinesky told me that—"

I suppose I was stopped dead in my tracks—so to speak!—because George's room was mostly a huge table covered with Lionel standard gauge HO track that ran over perfectly modeled hills and rills and suspension bridges, and through pastureland and woods and tunnels and realistic towns with main streets fronted by electrically lit municipal buildings, stores, and porched houses. It was like looking down from a cockpit, except there were too many trains chugging and spewing wisps of smoke as they rushed through miniature fields to miniature destinations. At least twenty brass-trimmed Lionel and American Flyer locomotives pulled blue, green, and yellow enamel cattle cars, boxcars, oil tank cars, coal cars, day coaches, Pullmans, baggage cars,

and bright red cabooses.

"You wanna try it?" George asked, as he pointed out a large black box that controlled the switching and speed; and I thought I said, "No," but there I was working the controls of the Blue Comet while George went into the kitchen to fix up drinks. Unlike the rest of his neighbors, he had a suite down here in the pit. I couldn't judge how many rooms he might have had.

For a few seconds, George's Blue Comet train set occupied all my attention because he had pushed all the rubber-tipped control levers over to #9 and the locomotives accelerated. They were chugging along so fast that they'd fly off the tracks when they hit the curves or smash into each other at the track switches. I pulled all the levers back, but not before a Cowen Comet Special locomotive pulling freight cars with their own magnetic lifting cranes jumped the track. Cars scattered across the table; although I prevented a few cars from falling, I couldn't reach the expensive, heavy black locomotive, which broke when it hit the floor.

"Good save," George said, returning with two whiskey glasses and a bottle.

"If that's your idea of a good save, you must have a lot of broken train sets."

George gestured toward two easy chairs placed around a table in the corner of the room. "What's the good of having things if you can't break them?"

There wasn't much I could say to that. We sat down, and he poured far too much whiskey into cut-glass

tumblers.

"That's why I'm down here. I broke too many things. So why give up a bad habit?"

"What did you break?" I asked.

"Ah... Confidences. The golden rule of silence. But only when I got drunk."

I tasted the whiskey, which was woody and bitter and good, and hefted the weight of the tumbler.

"You can *try* breaking that," George said, "but I'd drink up the contents first. You think it's crystal, don't you? Wrong, my boy. It's diamond...and probably enough to buy you the Ritz-Carlton in New York City, I would judge. But the boys have already told you that this mountain is one big diamond, didn't they? But that's probably about all they could tell you."

"What can *you* tell me?"

"Oh, probably everything."

"Can you tell me how to get out of here?" I asked.

"That's easy," he said, smiling and obviously enjoying himself hugely. "But you'll find out everything soon enough."

"How?"

He pointed upward, then poured himself another drink and topped mine up.

"For crying out loud, what are you getting at?"

"But don't break anything, 'cause he won't take you back."

"Who won't take me back where?"

"God won't take you back here."

Completely nuts, I thought.

After one more go-round with the trains, I left.

* * * * * * *

He probably was nuts.
But as I soon discovered, he was also probably right.

CHAPTER FOUR

It seemed like a dream, but, of course, it wasn't. I hadn't drunk very much, only a highball with Farley James and Keith Boardman in the library where we'd played a few games of mah-jongg after dinner. That might not sound like a very manly thing to do, but then none of that mattered in the pit. I'd become a veteran.

We shouted "Pung!" and "Chow!" and "Kong!" and swore blue murder as we rolled the dice and tried to build winning hands out of the inlaid ivory tiles. After about an hour, I started feeling queasy and headachy and cotton-mouthed, and so did Farley and Keith. We figured it was the food and blamed Snap Geraldson, who must have requested shit-on-a-shingle again—AKA tuna on toast—and the dumb-waiter in the dining room obliged.

So we dispersed and went to our rooms.

I fell asleep immediately, fell into the deep sleep of exhaustion, as though I was back in the war, flying mission after mission; and I dreamed that I was looking up at my ceiling, which glowed dimly like faraway neon; and it was like being a kid again and seeing faces and animals and buildings in the stucco

ceiling of my bedroom. Only now part of the ceiling was slowly floating down toward me, and two slaves dressed in white uniforms were standing on what might have been a scaffold platform. They were black angels, and they carried me up to heaven. I smelled sweat and ambergris and roses and

I dreamed that I would float upward forever...

* * * * * * *

As I woke up, blinking in the strong morning light, I could see ebony panels on tracks sliding open. Revealing formal gardens with stone hermae, geysering fountains, lamps, a marble wellhead, terra-cotta jars tall as a man, and statues of sylphs and mythical animals so lifelike that they almost seemed to move through the boughs and terraced pathways. My new chamber was now open to the world, and I could smell perfume and the richness of loamy soil. Beyond the gardens lay a small village of cottages massed around a church; but it was no ordinary church; it rose into the brittle blue sky like it was all of a steeple; and it was transparent as glass, proof that man could rise up and tear into the very fabric of Heaven.

"The gardens are indeed beautiful this morning, are they not, sir," said a man dressed in the same uniform as the men in my dream. He looked to be in his seventies, but he carried himself like an officer who was used to giving orders. His strong face and bald pate seemed polished; the wrinkles that radiated from his eyes and the corners of his thin mouth resembled fine

scrolling chiseled into mahogany.

"Yeath," I said, my mouth dry and swollen and tasting of iron. My tongue didn't seem to be working right; it filled my entire mouth and wouldn't get out of the way of my teeth.

I'd surely been drugged.

"Whey am I an' ha'ad I get hea?"

The old man smiled, as one would at a child, and said, "You're in the north bedroom of the guest suite. You're a guest of the master, and it's my privilege to serve you, Mr. Orsatti." I couldn't place his accent. It seemed Southern, but it had a certain crispness, a *wrongness*, as if an Englishman or German were speaking with a drawl.

I heard a rustling behind my bed, and although my head felt like it was half-filled with some vile-tasting, vile-smelling liquid, I managed to turn...and see a giant dressed in white like the old man.

"Don't give no never mind to Isaac, Mr. Orsatti. You can think of him as your shadow...or your own personal bodyguard, if you prefer. Isaac won't be a bother, as he understands no English... Now, *you've* got a big day today, sir. A bath to start the morning right, sir?"

My head began to clear and I found my voice. "Tell me what the hell I'm doing here?"

"It's up to the master alone to explain his intentions, sir. But I believe you're to give a recital in an hour."

"The master?"

"Master Jefferson, sir. Surely you know—"

"And you, what do *you* know?" I asked Isaac, who

stood as still as one of the statues in the garden and gazed at me disinterestedly.

"I told you, sir, he cannot understand you."

"Can't slaves understand English?"

"Sir, I am not in a position to advise...or to educate you. But I'm sure Master Jefferson will see to all your questions in his time."

"Are *you* a slave?" I asked. I would recite the Gettysburg Address to him if I had to.

"I have served Master Jefferson for many years, sir. Now would you prefer rosewater and a salt-water finish or a milk bath followed by warm water? Isaac will remove your pajamas."

I wasn't letting Isaac or anyone else near me.

I heard the old man sigh and nod his head, and then the bed tilted, and before I could gather my wits to grab hold of something, I was sliding toward the wall, pajamas and all. Drapes parted, as I slid down an incline into warm water. I heard myself shouting, but brought myself under control immediately. The chute folded back into the wall. I was in a sunken bath, the water warm as a womb; but swimming all around me— and above and below—were salt-water fish of every description: spiny fire fish, huge groupers, barramundi, mackerel, cod, orange-striped dragon fish, and there were jellyfish with long, almost transparent tentacles, a diamond-toothed moray eel, sea snakes, turtles, black spotted cuttlefish, and a hammerhead shark that was at least seven feet long.

The shark swam toward me, swam through the illu-

minated water.

Only a layer of crystal separated the shark from my feet, for my bathroom was inside an aquarium, and the great mass of water pressing against the walls cast shimmering, coruscating reflections everywhere. Then rain began to fall from the ceiling, and jets of rosewater and liquid soap bubbled into the bath while electric paddles churned the water into a blanket of sparkling soap bubbles. Music began playing, as if a chamber orchestra composed of mermaids were playing beside me.

The old man and Isaac stood on either side of the white marble sunken bath.

"My name is Robert," the old man said. "When you have completed your bath, Isaac will give you a rubdown and a shave and dress you. I will serve you breakfast in the sitting room," and with that he bowed and left.

Perhaps it was a combination of the drugs and warm bath, but—against my will—I found myself enjoying this warm, voluptuous kaleidoscope of a bath.

Nevertheless, I had the cold, dead feeling that I was being prepared for my last meal.

* * * * * * *

Washed, bathed, massaged, dressed, and fed steak filet and eggs and hills of fried potatoes on plates shaped out of layers of emerald and diamond and ruby, I was led—like a royal prisoner—through corridors and rooms with walls created entirely of diamonds and

other precious gems, through rooms where fire seemed to coruscate over walls and ceilings, through rooms composed of deep green crystal that could have held back the weight of an ocean with its dark, deep creatures, through elegant rooms, antique rooms, and rooms that might have been designed by Klee and Kandinsky to defy the normal rules of up and down. I walked over carpets of the rarest furs, glimpsed walls covered with paintings by Rubens, Caravaggio, da Vinci, Titian, Giotto, Manet, Monet, Poussin, Cézanne, and Miro, Picasso, Ernst, Gris, Demuth, and Modigliani. Marble creatures reached out to me: naiads, sylphs, satyrs, soldiers, gods, and goddesses by Michelangelo, Saint-Gaudens, Rodin, and Brancusi; and I was led up stairs cut into a huge, marble-veined extended hand.

Into a Baroque hall of mirrors that overlooked park-like grounds.

Hundreds of mirrors were set opposite windows and into the scrolled columns and archways. The high ceiling was curved, and painted angels gazed down from clouds in heaven upon gold and silver chairs and bejeweled trees. A forest of gold. Glades of diamonds. In keeping with this stone and jeweled forest was a grand piano that looked to be cut from a gigantic block of jade. Our feet clacked on the inlaid floor of this formal hall that seemed to extend into a finger-width arched door in the distance as Robert and Isaac led me to the piano.

Robert bowed and said, "I will leave you now, sir."

Isaac stood over me, and I was sure that, should I

stand up from the piano, he would force me back down onto the cushioned stool.

"And what am I to play?" I asked.

"I would think that would be up to you sir," Robert said, and, nodding to Isaac, he clattered away toward the far, perspective-shrunk doorway, his reflections creating an army of stiff, marching Roberts.

"And who am I to play to...?"

I sat before the translucent green piano, and began warming up by playing scales from Clementi's instruction book. Looking around the seemingly endless room, I couldn't see anyone except for Isaac, reflected in a dozen mirrors; he stood so still that I wondered if he even breathed. But I could *feel* other eyes watching me, and I remembered what crazy George Bernard had said about God not allowing me to return to my gilded prison. What was he planning for me, then? I wondered. Certainly Master Randolph Estes Jefferson wasn't going to take any chances with me, although I wondered...perhaps I *could* escape. I chuckled and looked around at this room constructed from dream and imagination. Would I *want* to escape?

But I could feel Isaac's presence pressing against me and knew I was freer in the pit. No matter, I was here to play, and if I failed Jefferson's test—if that was what it was—who knew what he might do. So I played, beginning with Chopin's *Waltz in G Flat*, then playing his préludes and nocturnes and études. I played Bach and Mozart and Beethoven. I expected *something* to happen. Someone besides Isaac to appear. Then I

began playing Erik Satie's piano works, which I loved: *Gymnopédies, Gnossiennes, Peccadilles importunes...* Satie the joker, the dissonant, the genius; and I heard a giggle behind me.

Saw reflections.

Phoebe stood before me, big as life, just as she stood beside and behind me, reflections in a myriad mirrors, a company of lovely, fragile, faun-like Phoebes looking awkward one instant and graceful the next. She wore a white gown, a silk scarf draped carelessly—or perhaps very carefully—over her shoulder, and a fetching bonnet with a red sash. Her eyes were indeed blue, her face was freckled, and she was the most beautiful creature I'd ever seen.

She said something to Isaac, which sounded like, "*Ra'ase, nah'ye haingwine heaightmuh*," and then she stood right by the piano and said, "Well, Mr. Paul Orsatti, you can certainly play, and I told Poppa that if he didn't bring you up out of that horrible place with those men, I'd never speak to him again. You're a genius, that's just what I told him, and I told him you'd be happy to teach me how to play the piano. I want to play as well as you, can you do that for me?"

I was about to tell her that I didn't know, but she said something else to Isaac, who looked sullenly down at the glassy floor.

"What did you say to him?" I asked.

"Just now, or before?" She looked steadily at me, and I could feel myself blushing. I don't know why, but she made me feel like I was sixteen and pimply

and gawky and trying to get up the courage to ask out the prom queen. She was just a wisp of a thing, her cheeks were freckled, and her curly blond hair stuck out from under her bonnet. Yet she seemed completely self-assured, as though she was accustomed to absolute obedience. And innocent. Perhaps it was the combination that unnerved me. Or perhaps I had just instantly fallen completely in love with her.

"I don't know," I said. "Both, I guess."

She giggled. "Well, I told him to calm himself down, that you probably weren't going to hurt me or kill me or anything like that." She backed away a step. "You're not, are you?"

"No, of course not."

"There, you see…? And then I told him…"

"Yes?"

"That's for me to know and you to find out," she said. "Now do you want to take me for a walk before you meet Poppa? He wants to have a talk with you."

"What about your friend Isaac?"

"Oh, don't worry about him. He'll keep out of the way," and she turned to him and glared. He quickly resumed looking at the floor.

"I'm Phoebe," she said as she led the way out of what she called the Mirror Gallery. Isaac followed, keeping a safe distance.

"I know your name."

"Ah, those awful men in the pit told you, did they." It wasn't a question. "I hate them."

"Why?"

"Because of what they say about me."

"And what is that?"

"That's for me to know."

I nodded. She was obviously younger than her years, but I couldn't help feeling attracted to her. I'd often been in the company of the rich and spoiled, and Phoebe was certainly the quintessential product of excess. Could she even imagine that there was another world out there, a world of people working twelve hours a day, haggling over pennies at the market, cooking their own food, sharing their possessions? Probably...no, definitely not.

"How did you know I could play the piano?" I asked.

"Well, because I heard you, that's how. Poppa can listen to everything those horrible men say down in the pit. And so can I, although if you tell Poppa that, I'll never speak to you again." We walked down a huge stone staircase and past the Neptune Pool that reflected the sun as a sheet of yellow light. "But you wouldn't care, would you?"

"About what?" I asked, overwhelmed by the sheer size of this place, by the formal gardens with statues as large as houses, by the pergola ahead, which was fashioned of crystal and gems and seemed to extend for a mile. And there was the chateau—the castle that connected to dozens of other buildings, each one of a different period, yet part of the perfect white, geometric whole—that was surrounded by pools the color of terra-cotta and marble constructions that resembled Greek and Roman ruins.

"You wouldn't care if I ever spoke to you again, would you, Mr. Paul Orsatti?" She sniffled, turning her head from me. "Well?"

"Of course, I would care."

"Why?"

"I don't know!"

"There, you see?" she said, but of course I didn't see.

"I listened to you play, even the night you got so drunk that the dumbbell with no eyebrows had to drag you to his room. I listened to you snore. Do you know how loud you snore? I'd do something about that if I were you."

I chuckled and asked if her father was able to see his prisoners as well as hear them. But Phoebe ignored that question...as though she hadn't heard it.

We walked past tennis courts, a reservoir, greenhouses, barracks, a zoo surrounded by marble lions, and then through the pergola to the edge of the formal gardens. Phoebe glanced back at Isaac every few minutes, and he would respectfully drop back several feet.

"I think it's all a lie," Phoebe said.

"What?" I asked.

"That the servants can't understand English. I think they've been tricking Poppa about that for years, and so does Uncle George."

"Uncle George?"

"You met him and played with his trains. That's what Poppa told me."

"Your *uncle* is in the pit?"

"Oh, yes," Phoebe said. "George Bernard Jefferson. He didn't tell you his last name, I imagine." She giggled. "He's always been in there. Well, practically always. But Poppa will tell you all about that. He tells everybody."

Everybody...? I thought.

"Would you like to kiss me now?" Phoebe asked, as we looked out at a herd of Master Jefferson's zebras grazing on a hill beyond the gardens. I said something inane about Isaac lurking behind us—which he was... and the moment passed.

Of course I wanted to kiss her. But she looked so vulnerable...and she was so young.

"Do you hear that?"

"What?"

"Airplanes, I think. Listen—"

Sure enough, I could hear engines. But I couldn't see anything in that eggshell sky, which was the exact color of Phoebe's eyes.

CHAPTER FIVE

An alarm sounded and a chill caught the air as we made our way back to the castle, which Phoebe called *Adamas*. She told me with breathless conviction that the king of France hadn't lived in anything half as nice, and she ought to know, she said, because Poppa had all the plans of the greatest castles in the world, and he made sure that his was the best. She was excited about reaching the roof garden so we could watch the airplanes through the telescope there.

Although she hurried to the castle, she was not in the least afraid. Isaac tried to say something to her, but she had only to shout something quick and guttural at him and he fell back behind us, properly cowed.

Then a porcine, well-dressed young man flanked by what I took for two slaves caught up with us by the Roman ruins beside the pool. He was nervous and out of breath, and kept looking at the sky as if lightning were going to strike him down at any second. Just ahead was a marble staircase that led to the western exposures of one of the buildings that adjoined the chateau. I could see a glint of metal: the telescope mounted on the embrasure.

"Father sent me to find you," he said, out of breath. "You won't believe how angry he is. You're supposed to be in the bunkers, and not legging around with *him*." He meant me, and his eyebrows knitted together and his face got all scrunched up when he said "him." I couldn't help but smile.

"You won't even get to keep him until September, if you act like that," the young man continued. "And that's *exactly* what Father said. I didn't make it up."

The alarm sounded again.

"Now come on, for crying out loud, or do you want to get killed out here?"

"Those airplanes are probably just mail carriers, like always," Phoebe said. "And mail carriers don't carry bombs. But they're all gone now."

She cocked her head, obviously listening for the sound of airplane engines. Everything was quiet, but for the wind.

"You see, false alarm. All that trouble for nothing... and I *was* coming back."

"Well, you can tell that to Father," the young man said.

"You're not my boss, Mr. Near Beer."

The young man blushed at that, and Phoebe said, "Mr. Orsatti, this is my brother, Morgan."

Morgan gave me a slight nod, then shouted something at Isaac; but I couldn't understand a word.

"Isaac had nothing to do with it," Phoebe said. "It was my idea. And if you dare say one word—"

I heard the sudden drone of an engine, and then the

deafening, bone-shaking *stucka-stucka* of anti-aircraft guns, which were mounted on the castle fortifications above.

There was another burst...and another.

"You see?" Morgan screamed at Phoebe, and he grabbed her. But she broke free. Isaac stepped over to her, as if to intervene. The guns fired again. I heard a distant explosion, but couldn't see any airplanes— the castle blocked the view. One of Jefferson's slaves shouted something to Isaac, who looked nervously at Phoebe and then at me, before running after Morgan and his fellows.

"Morgan is such a flat tire," Phoebe said. "And I'll bet you ten thousand dollars right now that those enemy airplanes don't have any guns." She paused, then explained, "According to Poppa, everybody is the enemy. And so Morgan is always so-oh afraid we're going to get bombed. I know that Poppa scares the bunk out of him about it to make a man out of him, but Morgan is just a flat tire."

I followed her up the marble staircase, across a patio, and up several more staircases to the roof garden. I could see Jefferson's slaves manning the anti-aircraft guns, which were quiet now. Ghostly pink billowing clouds were filling up the sky like suds in a bathtub. From the position of the sun, I could see it was late afternoon. But how could that be? I must have slept through the morning.

I stared at an oily trail of black smoke left by a plane that had been shot out of the sky. But I could also hear

the distant thrumming of an engine. Perhaps it was one of Jefferson's. Or perhaps one of the intruders had escaped into the swollen pink and purple curtain of storm clouds. Phoebe tossed her bonnet onto a wrought iron chair and looked through the brass telescope, swinging it around so hard, it was a wonder she could see *anything*.

"There it is," she said. "Right over...there... Poppa's guns got it. See the smoke in the canyon? Something's burning. Positively. But I can't make out very much. I can't see for jellybeans without my glasses. Here, you try." She pulled away from the telescope, brushing my face with her curly hair, and I could smell her perfume, lilac sweet and damp. I looked through the eyepiece. There was indeed a plane burning. I couldn't see it well through the smoke, but it looked like a Curtiss Jenny. I wondered if the pilot made it to safety and tried to cover the area by moving the telescope around, but Phoebe became impatient and insisted that I return it to her immediately. After a time she said, "I can't see anything. Do you want to bet on the pilot?"

"What do you mean?"

"A thousand dollars that Poppa's slaves find him alive and put him in the pit." She shrugged. "If he's dead, you win."

"I wouldn't make such a bet," I said. "And I certainly don't have a thousand dollars."

Phoebe pulled a magnificent diamond and ruby ring from her index finger and slipped it onto my pinkie. "That should cover your side of the bet." She smiled

mischievously and said, "Now we're engaged."

"I can't accept this," I said, handing her back the ring.

"Perhaps I made a mistake about you, Mr. Paul Orsatti."

"It's very beautiful, but I don't think your father—"

"He won't care. He's going to be too upset to care about anything, which means he won't be bothering too much about you." She took my hand, slipped the ring over my finger again.

"What do you mean?"

"There was another plane," Phoebe said. "Couldn't you hear it?"

"Yes, but I thought it might have been your father's."

Phoebe laughed at that, a soft, sexy, whispery laugh. "Not unless he was flying it. Or Morgan." She laughed again. "Or Uncle George."

"You've got plenty of...slaves."

She seemed astonished. "Why, you couldn't allow a slave to fly an airplane."

"Why not?"

"Because...you just couldn't. But it doesn't matter. Poppa will surely find out who was flying that plane and what company he worked for and fix it all up. He always fixes everything up."

"You mean he'll have him killed."

She shook her head and looked genuinely hurt. "Poppa's an honorable man. He'll have him brought back here to live and give him everything he could want. We don't just go around murdering people, you

know." When I didn't say anything, she asked, "Are you sorry?"

"About what?"

"What you said about my father."

"Yes, of course. I'm sorry."

She turned back to me and asked, "Well, do you still want to kiss me?"

"I never said I wanted to kiss you."

But against all judgment—of course—I did.

* * * * * * *

Phoebe and I lay in bed. It was evening, and the garden was a fantasia of fairy lights. A sweetly scented breeze wafted in through the balcony, shadows and pale, milky lights played over a wall-sized Flemish tapestry of Neptune standing upon a shell and creating a horse of air with his trident. The walls were covered with blue brocade from Scalamandre, and the gilded wood ceiling glowed as if lit by fireflies. Phoebe was curled up beside me, and we were wrapped in smooth satin sheets as blue as the brocade.

"You see, everything is perfect," Phoebe said. "I knew it would be. I always know."

"Ah, so you always lure lonely prisoners into your den to have your way with them, is that it?"

"Exactly so." After a pause, she said, "How could you even imagine I would have anything to do with anyone else?"

There was nothing to say to that, so I enjoyed being close to her, feeling her smooth shoulder and slipping

my hand down to caress her small breast. She was thin and long and smooth and as perfect as I had imagined.

"Well, just in case it might interest you, I've never had anything to do with anyone down there"—I knew she meant the pit—"or anyone who Poppa has brought to visit."

"So your father does have guests here," I said. "Doesn't he worry about security?" For an instant, Phoebe seemed to be nonplussed, but then she giggled and said, "Poppa worries about everything."

"What if they told their friends? Why—"

"They're very rich," Phoebe said. "Not nearly as rich as we are, of course, but they're worth quite a boodle, you can count on that. And Poppa could just as easily make their shares in the stock market go up or down. He can make it do whatever he wants. But you, Mr. Paul Rudolph Valentino Piano-player, you're like a big dog with a bone, aren't you? Now, do you *really* want to talk about Poppa's friends, or..."

She was quite persuasive; and I was indeed, in all respects, like a dog with a bone. "What was all that business about not getting to keep me until September?" I insisted. "What did your brother mean by that?"

She drew away from me and pulled the sheets up to her neck, as though she were wearing them as a nightgown. "You got what you want, so thanks for the buggy ride. And now you want to play twenty questions."

I tried to put my arm around her, but she turned away, taking most of the sheets with her. It suddenly felt cold in the room.

"I didn't mean to hurt your feelings." I said. "I—"

"Then say you're sorry."

"I'm sorry."

She unraveled herself from the sheets and turned toward me. "I'm coming out in London in September. I'll be presented at court, and I'll meet King George. He's also a friend of Poppa's. Now does *that* answer your question?"

Of course it didn't; but I would bide my time. I nodded.

"Then you may have your way with me again."

But that wasn't to be either because there was a sharp knock on the door, followed by the booming voice of God.

"I'm not dressed, Poppa," Phoebe said sweetly, sitting up in the bed. She seemed to be talking to the polychrome sculpture of Saint John that was positioned beside the paneled door. "I'll meet you down in the library." She looked at me and shrugged.

"You'll open this door right now, young lady!"

"No I *won't!*"

I started to get up. I could grab my clothes, perhaps hide; but Phoebe said, "Don't be goofy. He'll go away in a minute. Absolutely-positively."

Then I heard Jefferson say something incomprehensible in a low voice—most likely, he was speaking to one of his slaves.

I was right.

I should have known better than to listen to Phoebe. Now it was too late.

A key turned in the lock, Robert pushed the great door open, and Master Randolph Estes Jefferson, dressed impeccably in formal eveningwear—white tie and tails—walked into the room. Phoebe was a blur rushing into the adjoining bathroom; it was a wonder she didn't slip on the blue, diamond-smooth floor. She slammed the door shut and left me to face the music by myself. There was nothing I could do but pull the sheets around me. My clothes were strewn across the floor.

Passion had certainly taken precedence over foresight.

"Do you see what happens, Robert, when you leave guests unattended?" Master Jefferson spoke to his slave in English.

Robert nodded and looked at me as if I were the wayward child and he was the parent.

"Well, good evening, Mr. Orsatti," Jefferson said. "I see that you have already provided my daughter with her first lesson. I will expect you to attend to my daughter's musical education with as much ardor as you seem to have displayed here tonight." He lifted my undershorts with the toe of his polished leather spats and then kicked them across the room. "And I am expecting to see a marked improvement in her proficiency at the piano, Mr. Orsatti. In September, she will give a recital at Carnegie Hall. It's all arranged."

"Sir, don't you think that's a bit, er, premature...?"

Jefferson gave me a genial smile, his ruddy, fleshy face the picture of cheerfulness, his eyes as hard as the

diamond mountain below us. "Wouldn't you say *this* is premature, sir?" he said, looking around the room, indicating my situation with a simple turn of his head. Then he nodded to Robert, who picked up my scattered clothes and laid them out neatly on the corner of the bed.

"You look perplexed, Mr. Orsatti," Jefferson continued. "Did you expect I would have you beaten? Or killed? Or thrown back into the pit with your colleagues? No, you're Phoebe's guest now. And Phoebe is a woman of the '20s. Why, she's practically emancipated."

"*Practically* emancipated?" Phoebe asked, opening her bathroom door a crack and peering out. The light behind her transformed her curly hair into a halo.

"Well, maybe you'd prefer to leave school and go to work for Mrs. Millie Scotch Barker and her suffragettes," Jefferson said. "But this is none of your business, young lady. You're taking your bath, are you not? While poor Mr. Orsatti must make his own introductions."

"For your information, her name isn't Millie Scotch Barker. It's Abby Scott Baker, and in case you've been too busy to notice, Poppa, we've won the right to vote."

"*You* don't have the right to vote, nor do I think you'd care to be poor."

"I know poor people at school," Phoebe said.

"Ah, yes, those poor girlfriends of yours who can't afford to keep their own staffs of servants.

"Well, I know Mr. Orsatti."

"Ah, yes, Mr. Orsatti, whom you're going to make as rich as Croesus, isn't that so?"

"If you have no objections, Poppa," Phoebe said meekly, then closed the bathroom door.

Jefferson chuckled and said, "Well, Croesus had better dress for dinner, hadn't he? When Robert is finished with you, Mr. Orsatti, he'll bring you to my library, and I will explain everything before we join the ladies. No, better yet, Robert, bring him to the theater. Do you like moving pictures, Mr. Orsatti...?"

Without waiting for an answer, Jefferson left, and Robert introduced me to my new bodyguard, Wordsworth, who had been waiting like a good foot soldier in the wood-paneled lobby. I learned that Isaac was being punished for a dereliction of duty, and I would not see him again. I wondered if *anyone* would ever see him again.

As Robert and Wordsworth escorted me out of the room, I could hear the faint splashing of water and Phoebe singing in a sweet, yet raucous voice—"Who's Sorry Now?"

* * * * * * *

Scrubbed down like a horse after a race, perfumed, pomaded, and dressed in evening clothes, I sat in the richly cushioned maroon seat beside Jefferson and watched Fatty Arbuckle and Buster Keaton slap each other across the screen.

Jefferson's "theater" was more magnificent than any movie house I'd ever been in. Scarlet damask lined the

walls, and the thirty-foot ceiling was supported by huge gold caryatids holding dimly glowing ruby lamps. As the moving picture flickered before me like a dream, I sipped Napoleon brandy and smoked a sweet cigar rolled in the Haymarket district of New York City. But the butterfly collar that Robert had snapped around my neck was so heavily starched that I felt like I was wearing sandpaper.

"I think all that business about Fatty raping that actress and all is a lot of hooey," Jefferson said in a whisper, although there was no one but his manservants and us in the theater. This was certainly a place that inspired awe, a church for the brightly lit images that towered before us in profound silence. This was the perfect temple for the new gods that were so much larger than life and above the sound and the fury, beyond boredom or smell or homely sound. We might laugh at their antics, but *they* would have the last laugh and live forever. However, being here in this sumptuous palace atop a mountain of pure diamond, it would be easy to imagine that *we* were the new gods.

"Even if he did have a bit of fun with her," Jefferson continued, "it would have been her fault, not his. He didn't force her to stay at his hotel. He didn't force her to stay there for two of God's long days. And now the poor soul is blacklisted and can't make a moving picture because that stupid woman ruptured her bladder, probably from being loaded to the plimsoll."

"Well, she did die from it," I said as we watched Buster Keaton being struck by a sack of flour. Keaton

absorbed the shock as if he had been struck by a hanky. I'd seen *Butcher Boy*, although I can't say it was one of my favorites. But Jefferson howled with laughter.

After he calmed down, he said, "The court cleared him of all charges, and the jury said that a great injustice had been done to him."

"It did take three trials."

"I wouldn't care if it took a hundred trials. He was completely exonerated."

"I'm not sure that—"

"Are you going to continue to argue with me?" Jefferson asked. His voice was soft, mellifluous, and menacing.

"No, of course not. I apologize."

"From what Phoebe tells me, you're good at that." He laughed, whether at me or Fatty Arbuckle's antics, I couldn't tell; but he patted my arm, thus preserving my...dignity. "Perhaps I should get into the film business. What do you think? Give Arbuckle a second chance?"

"The press and public seem to hate him," I said.

He pulled on his cigar, belched a huge cloud of smoke, and said, "I can fix the press. And I can guarantee that the public will love him. I'll bet you a thousand dollars. Is it a bet?"

"I've already had a conversation like this once with your daughter, sir. I don't really *have* a thousand dollars."

"Ah, but you've got a new ring, haven't you?"

"I think we'd both be in the doghouse if I lost her

ring to you on a wager."

Jefferson seemed to like that because he put his arm around me, waved the porter over to fill my snifter with more brandy, insisted that I stop acting like a teetotaler, and told me the "improbable but true" story of the Jefferson family.

When he finished, I asked, "Why are you telling me all this?" I had become more and more nervous as he spoke because...I already knew too much.

But he just handed our crystal—or perhaps they were diamond—snifters to one of his servants and said, "Because you're part of the family now, Paul.

"Shall we join the ladies...?"

CHAPTER SIX

Randolph Estes Jefferson was no relative of Thomas Jefferson.

Nor was he the scion of any distinguished lineage. His father Frances Tiberio Jefferson did, however, settle in Shadwell, Albemarle County, Virginia, where the third president of the United States was born and grew up; and he claimed to be a distant cousin of "Thomas," who also had a reputation of being able to talk a tree out of its roots. Frances won a medal for "World's Greatest Liar" at the Great Albemarle Fair. Like Thomas, he was a states' rights man and distinguished himself in the War of Yankee Aggression by rising to the rank of Colonel. He was too robust to succumb to the diseases that routed both the northern and southern armies, and rose quickly through the thinning ranks.

After the war, he took his pay and his gift of gab and became the most successful auctioneer in Albemarle County; but he was too restless for that.

It happened that he found twenty-five "orphans," ex-slaves still living on a played-out plantation. Their owners had put the plantation up for sale and left for Europe. The men and women left behind spoke high

German, had developed their own, unique dialect, and didn't know that the North had won the war and that they were no longer...slaves. They were starving and Frances fed them, gained their trust, and promised them wealth and a piece of land out west.

However, he neglected to explain that they were emancipated.

And so Frances left the Thomas Jefferson Auctioneers & Feed Company to his brother. His plan was to buy twenty parcels of cheap Montana land in the names of his new wards and start a cattle and sheep farm. But that was not to be because, after a series of misadventures, all he had left were his orphans; and they were starting to have doubts about the master who could do no wrong.

In fact, they would have probably killed him if he had not gotten lost in the mountains and shot a squirrel that happened to have a perfect diamond the size of a pebble in its mouth. That pebble would be worth a hundred thousand dollars. He went back to his camp and told his orphans that he had discovered a cache of "rhinestones" that could be mined "for a few dollars." Since none of the slaves had ever seen a diamond, much less owned one, they agreed that they could dig out enough stones to get back sufficient money to buy homesteads.

Leaving his miners to continue their work, he took a valise of diamonds to Billings; but he underestimated their value and a jeweler, flabbergasted at the size and quality of one of the smallest stones, tried to have

Frances arrested. Frances went to New York, where he started another furor; this with only one stone, which a dealer of consequence believed might have been part of the Duvergier Diamond, said to have been stolen by a French soldier from the eye of an idol. The Duvergier had been cut into twenty-one stones, which ranged from less than a carat to eighty carats, and The World's Greatest Liar did not dispute the opinion that *his* diamond might have been cut from the same venerable stone.

After several weeks, Frances was several hundred thousand dollars richer. But he had to leave New York, as the metropolitan police were now looking for him. The diamond market was in chaos. Some said that the world's largest diamonds were somehow being cut up and "dumped by a "syndicate." These new stones *had* to be cut from great diamonds such as the Orloff, the Koh-i-nor, the Akbar Shah, the Dudley, and even the Cullinan—which became part of the crown jewels— because they were too big to be anything else. Madness had replaced logic. Would-be prospectors were rushing to Scranton, Pennsylvania, and Southampton, Long Island—and the yellow rags kept proclaiming new locations where diamonds had "just been discovered."

Indeed, The World's Greatest Liar had found what was undoubtedly the world's largest diamond...a solid and perfect mountain of diamond; and he realized that he would have to be careful, lest he devalue the world market.

He sent for his brother to manage the mine and left

for a tour of the world. Carefully, he sold his diamonds. He used pseudonyms, forged passports. He lived like a criminal on the lam, yet he sold his stones to emperors, kings, criminals, sultans, and mercantile barons; his diamonds became invested with their own history and myth, as if they had been in circulation for hundreds, if not thousands of years.

In a few years, Frances was worth millions.

In a few more years, he was worth billions.

And he married a Spanish beauty; had two sons, Randolph and George; convinced his slaves that the South had indeed won the war, and that all was once again right with the world; murdered his brother, who became too generous with the family fortune and "talked out of school"; and dedicated himself to protecting his family and consolidating his fortune.

Randolph, being a chip off the old block, also invested widely and wisely; saw to the construction of his castle on the mountain; married a woman from Braga, his mother's village near the west coast of Spain; sired a son and two daughters; and being kinder and gentler than Frances, merely imprisoned his overly generous and voluble brother, rather than murdering him.

Thus was I introduced to the secrets of the family while titans who had assumed the shapes of Fatty Arbuckle and Buster Keaton beat and kicked each other in joyous, rapturous revenge.

CHAPTER SEVEN

It was like being invited to dinner in a cathedral, perhaps because great pennons hung from the high, gilded wood ceilings and paintings of winged cherubs and Rubenesque angels gazed down upon the guests, as though the heavenly host itself were in attendance. Perhaps it was the plundered sixteenth-century choir stalls, or the flickering candles and the altar of a table spread with linen and silver and gold. The plates and glassware seemed to be composed of layers of ruby, sapphire, emerald, opal, and diamond. Muted colors and pure, prismatic reflections met my eyes wherever I looked, and the Persian tile upon which I stood seemed to have infinite depth, as if this great room was floating stock-steady upon extraordinarily deep water. Servants glided in and out, as though stepping through shadows, and I could hear the clear but distant strains of Vivaldi's *The Four Seasons*. I tried to locate the music, but could not.

Randolph Jefferson stood at the head of the long table and motioned me toward a chair beside Phoebe, who was dressed like a blond angel in white chiffon. Beside Phoebe, and facing Jefferson at the other end

of the table, sat a beautiful dark-haired woman wearing a black chiffon evening dress. I thought it particular that, except for a gold wedding band, she wore no jewelry. She looked like she could have been in mourning. To Jefferson's right was Morgan, and beside Morgan was a homely brown-haired girl in a stylish green evening outfit that somehow seemed larger than she was.

"Paul, allow me to introduce you to Giroma, my wife." I bowed, and the woman in black held out her hand to me. I wasn't sure whether I was expected to kiss it or formally shake it, so I decided upon the latter. She seemed pleased, but then she turned away from me, as though impatient to return to her own thoughts.

"And my son, Morgan, who tells me y'all met under rather unexpected circumstances." Jefferson gave Morgan a cold, disapproving look and then introduced me to Marion, his eldest daughter, who was still being overwhelmed by her green evening dress. Perhaps I had been too hasty in describing Marion as homely. She had the same features as Phoebe, but they were slightly...crooked. What seemed like perfection in one sister was bland and uncomely in the other.

"Sit down," Phoebe whispered to me. "You look like you just stepped on your own foot." Marion giggled at that and, embarrassed, I sat down.

We made small talk throughout dinner, all seven courses, and Phoebe was winsome and witty and wickedly pressed her leg against my thigh. I asked about the music, wondering how many more musicians—indeed,

how many other "guests" might be on the grounds—only to learn that the sweet music was being reproduced by an electrical phonograph that used a new Panatrope loud-speaker.

"It's the bass that fools you, Paul," Jefferson said. "It's big as life, don't you agree? The old orthophonic machines aren't a patch on this one. The diaphragm of the loudspeaker is coil-driven, the acetate records are finely grooved, and the stylus is diamond, of course. The Victor Talking Machine Company will be bringing out a version like this...sometime in the next four or five years, I would suppose." Jefferson seemed very pleased with himself.

I nodded, unsettled that I was the only guest. Phoebe's sister Marion must have been reading my mind because she complained, "It's not fair, Poppa, that Phoebe always receives special treatment. She's coming out before me, and I'm older. And you've allowed *her* to have company. I haven't had *any* company this summer." While Phoebe's voice was smooth, dulcet, Marion's was whiny.

"Phoebe has company for a reason," Jefferson said. "Would you have her give her concert unprepared?"

"She's never going to be prepared," Marion said, looking defiantly at Phoebe, who stared assiduously into her jeweled plate, as though she could move the broccoli by the mere power of her gaze. "She can't play the piano any better than I can, yet you've bought Carnegie Hall for her."

"I did no such thing," Jefferson said. "She was

invited to play, as you might have been if you had applied yourself."

"She only wanted to play piano because I did. And y'all went gaga over *her* and couldn't even be bothered with me."

"That's not true."

"It is too. It's because Phoebe is a liar. She lies to all of you, and you believe everything she tells you. It's not fair, it's just not fair."

"Are you quite finished?"

"I'm sick of being here all by myself."

"You have your family here, or is that of no importance to you?"

Marion shook her head and said, "It's not fair."

"I'll spend time with her, Poppa," Phoebe said. "I will, Marion, I promise."

"That's the bunk!" Marion said to her father. "She's a liar."

"Morgan, what do you have to say?" Jefferson asked.

"Don't know, I—"

"She's your sister, and it's your responsibility to take care of her, isn't that right?"

"Yes...I suppose, but—"

"Well, I've decided that you should follow up our little problem with the pilot who got away from us," Jefferson said. "What do you think of that? It's time you proved yourself to be a man."

"What do you want me to do?" Morgan asked.

"More to the point, what do *you* think you should do?"

"I dunno...go find him, I guess."

"And what does that have to do with me?" Marion asked. "You see, that's just what I mean. I'm invisible."

"Not at all," Jefferson said. "You're the eldest. Perhaps I should send *you* out to test your mettle instead of Morgan."

"Perhaps you should send *me*," Phoebe said. "Mr. Orsatti could protect me."

"Indeed he could," Jefferson said. "Indeed he could," and they exchanged teasing looks, as if they had rehearsed this little skit—as if Mother and Morgan and Marion were out, and only Poppa and Phoebe were in.

And I soon found out where I stood in their dangerous little universe.

* * * * * * *

"Oh, Poppa wouldn't send either one of them to the grocer for a loaf of bread," Phoebe confided to me as we stood on the artificially lit, glaucous-green lawn that seemed to roll on forever into the night.

Fireflies pulsed in the perfumed air. I held her cool hand; and I must admit that against all logic and experience and plain good sense, I was head over heels in love. It wasn't about what kind of a person Phoebe might be—how smart, immature, spoiled, and selfish she was. I knew her for a brat, and probably as dangerous as her father. Perhaps more dangerous. But she was...perfect. The sound of her voice was perfect, the way her eyes narrowed when she was thinking

was perfect, her smell, the cast of her hair, the way her eyebrows arched, the curl of her mouth—all absolute perfection. I was smitten, but at least I had the presence of mind to conceal the extent of my ardor...or so I thought, anyway. In fact, I was as transparent as the goblet I had been drinking from at dinner.

"I'm surprised that he lets either one of them go to school," she continued.

"You don't like Morgan and Marion very much, do you?"

"*Au contraire*, I love them both to pieces. But would *you* let them out of your sight?"

"I'd rather not let you out of my sight."

She giggled and pulled me to a copse of trees that were silver and shadow in the dim, flickering lamplight. She sat down, her back against the bole of an elm.

"You'll catch cold on the damp ground," I said.

"Poppa will go alone," she said, as though talking to herself. "He won't take Morgan. I'll bet you a thousand..."

"Don't start that again."

"Did Poppa try to make a bet with you?"

"Why do you ask?"

She twirled the ring on my finger...the ring she had given me. "I expect he noticed my ring. Well, did he?"

"Did he notice...?"

"No, did he make you put it up for collateral?"

"I would never bet your ring."

"Good for you," Phoebe said. "Poppa likes you."

"He didn't suggest sending *me* to find your flier."

"But he did take you out of the pit."

"Because you asked him to."

"And you'd just better remember that," she said, and then allowed me to fumble with her clothes, caress her breasts, kiss her in all the delicious, unmentionable places, and finally make love to her. Everything was rustling and whispering and breathing, and when we were finished—and still half-dressed—she said, "You haven't said you love me."

Caught off guard, I just smoked my cigarette.

"And you didn't offer *me* a cigarette."

I gave her the cigarette, which she smoked, inhaling deeply. She didn't cough…she just cleared her throat, as though she were about to give a formal speech. "Well, are you going to say it?"

"How could you be sure I'd mean it?"

"Because I know you do."

"And what about you?"

"Do you think I'd let you do what you just did if I didn't?"

I knew better than to fall into that trap.

"I love you," I said, trying to arouse her again.

"I know you do," Phoebe said, surrendering, or pretending to.

"But there is something else."

Phoebe pulled away and watched me.

"You've had company here before. Your sister said as much."

"Ah, so we're on that old stick again."

"Well, I still can't get what your father said out of my mind."

"And what would that be?" Phoebe sat up again and leaned against the tree. Her blouse was open, her hair was mussed, and I must admit I could not imagine anyone being more beautiful, alluring, and piquant.

"That unless you behave, you won't be able to keep me until September."

"Morgan said that, remember? And he lies."

"I need to know," I said, insistent.

"I've only had one friend from school ever visit me for vacation," Phoebe said. "A girlfriend. And you wouldn't have liked her, anyway."

"Why?"

"You just wouldn't. *I* didn't like her very much. I..."

"Yes...?"

"That's all. Now, are you done with your Twenty Questions?"

"Does your sister usually have guests?" I asked.

"So now it's Forty Questions, is it," Phoebe said, and she buttoned her blouse.

I felt the sudden distance between us, but I couldn't stop. "Well, does she?"

"Yes, this is the first summer she's been alone. Poppa's punishing her."

"Why?"

"Because she has a big mouth. She takes after Uncle George." She looked around, and although she didn't act nervous, I knew she was. I could feel it radiating from her.

"Your father doesn't let your guests return home, does he." That was a statement, not a question.

"What do you want from me?" Phoebe asked.

"The truth."

"Why? Will it make you free?"

I waited for an answer.

Phoebe looked directly at me as she spoke, as if the truth would be a reproach. "You're right...Father doesn't allow the guests to return home."

Then he imprisons them, like he did me?"

"No," she whispered, watching, studying me. "That wouldn't be fair to the family."

"The family?"

"To us."

"Why?"

"Because we'd feel terrible. Mother would have a breakdown. She's had one already."

"So you *murder* them?"

She flinched at that, but kept looking at me, unafraid yet vulnerable. "There is no—there is really no other choice. Marion and Morgan need friends. And Poppa is too considerate to force them to be hermits."

"Considerate? I—"

"You'd think we starved and tortured them," Phoebe said. "Invited guests are shown every courtesy. They have the best time of their lives—good company, good food, the best quarters, and Marion and Morgan and Mother shower them with presents. Whatever they fancy they get, and when their time comes, they simply go to sleep. It's really very pleasant, I would imagine.

It really is... It always happens in August or September, but Marion and Morgan never know exactly when. It's easier for them, that way."

"And what about their poor families?" I asked, aghast.

"We explain that they caught typhus and passed away, and Poppa *always* sends flowers."

"How lovely. And when is my time going to be, hey? This month or next."

"Well, you do have to give me lessons for my recital," Phoebe said. She was playing with me, yet I was convinced that she had told me the truth. Jefferson would never allow anyone to give up his secrets. It was a miracle that he allowed his brother George to live—perhaps he was a trifle sentimental.

I got up to leave, and she said, "If you go now, I'll never speak to you again."

"What's the difference?"

"What's the *difference*...? Do you seriously believe I would bring my friends here, knowing Poppa wasn't going to allow them to leave?"

"Well, you have. *I'm* your guest. Or rather your victim."

"Go fly a kite! You were going to rot down there in the pit."

"But I wouldn't be about to be murdered. Is it this week or next?"

"I wouldn't allow Poppa to murder you. He agreed that when you're finished tutoring me for my recital, you'll go back in the pit. So there! I wouldn't kill

anybody. Not even you."

I could hear her breathing falter like she was going to cry, but I persisted.

"But you have, haven't you? You've probably had as many guests as Marion. Or Morgan. Or your mother, for that matter."

"Mother never has guests, neither does Poppa," Phoebe said. "They allow us to have guests because there's no other choice. Mother stays by herself and barely speaks, or haven't you noticed? She lost her best friends, and couldn't stand to lose any more."

"It's disgusting."

"We're not like other people. We can't live like they do. If we could, we would. And for your information, Mister Know-it-all, when I found out what Poppa had to do, I refused to invite anybody else ever again. I'm content to read and enjoy music and walk in the gardens. Alone."

"That's very white of you."

"Thank you."

With that, I turned and walked away.

Half-dressed and shoeless, she caught up with me.

"Paul, do you really believe I could abide you being killed or put back with those other…men?"

"I don't really know," I said. "I would guess that you could."

"I love you. I didn't know that when I saw you in the pit, or when I heard you play the piano like a genius. And Poppa would never hurt anyone in the family."

"I'm your piano teacher, Phoebe. I'm not in the

family."

"But you will be when we're married...."

CHAPTER EIGHT

Phoebe was, of course, correct. Her father left the mountain by himself to take care of business. It seemed that eight pilots had already been murdered by his agents, yet none of Jefferson's sources could be absolutely sure that the right pilot had been dispatched. Jefferson was going to take matters into his own hands and direct his army of spies, scouts, facilitators, lawyers, bankers, and mercenaries to find the "conspirators," wipe them out, and smooth over the facts so that no one would ever recollect that anything odd or untoward had ever occurred. Whether Jefferson was a good general, a coward, or just foolhardy, I couldn't say. But when the shooting started and all hell broke loose, he should have been present.

However, I'm getting a bit ahead of myself...

* * * * * * *

The next few weeks were bliss. Just Phoebe and me. There were long, languorous hours in the mirror gallery, the afternoon sun a dusty-golden mist filling the long, arched room as Phoebe concentrated on her music...and me. She was going to dedicate her recital

to me and play a selection of my favorite piano works by Erik Satie. I tried to talk her into playing a selection of Chopin's waltzes and preludes and explained that Satie's music was absurdist and humorous and only seemingly simple, but she was not to be dissuaded. The hours of practice were punctuated by lovemaking and champagne lunches on the balcony. She disappeared the slaves. They were to be invisible, yet at her beck and call, as it should be, she said; and she was summer itself. Every day another Phoebe appeared, as though by magic. Sometimes she was an Egyptian queen in evening gown. Sometimes a chic matron wearing cloche hats and "Coco" Chanel skirts and pullovers and suits designed specifically for her and no one else. She could be "Flapper Jane" with heavy makeup and oiled hair and whiskey on her breath, or an athletic fresh-faced beauty in pleated skirt and blue bandeau.

And so the days passed, each delicious, each one only slightly different from those before. We swam in a green pool illuminated by ivory lamps under a ceiling of hammered gold. Surrounded by marble Roman sarcophagi and statues of Sekhmet, the Egyptian goddess of war and destruction, we made love. We had dinner with the family and made small talk; we hardly saw Morgan and Marion, who were sullen and secretive, as if they were privy to something we were not.

I found out what *that* was all about a few nights later.

* * * * * * *

Although Phoebe and I made love every night, we

slept in our respective rooms. "When we're married, you can stay the night," she said; and, indeed, by midnight I would be so exhausted from the rigors of the night—and the day—that I would fall into a deep, satisfying sleep, only to be awakened by Robert with breakfast on a gold tray and the bright, pure light of another perfect morning.

But on the night when all hell broke loose, I was dreaming of the boys in the pit. I was back there with them, and so was Joel, who was dead, of course. But in the dream, we were all dead—except Phoebe and old man Jefferson and Morgan and Marion, who were all dressed in formal finery and standing on the golf course above us by the grated opening of the pit. Jefferson was praying for us and mixing up the part about dust to dust, and then Phoebe started crying while her brother and sister began shoveling dirt into the pit to bury us. There would be no more golden days and luminous nights with Phoebe, no more lovemaking in Jefferson's forests of gold and glades of diamonds, no more Bach or Beethoven, nor the ironic mockings of Satie. I could smell grass and rot and decay, the Paris perfume of Phoebe mixed with her sweet sweat as the clumps of black soil fell on top of us. Black rain. Phoebe's tears, tapping, dropping like soft leather heels on marble.

I choked. I couldn't breathe. I—

Woke up to scuffing, whispering, creaking. Then the click of the diamond doorknob being turned, the sighing of the door. I didn't wait to determine who the intruders were because I was sure they were going to

try to kill me, just as they killed all the other guests. But I couldn't escape without somehow getting past them. Unless…

I felt for the button on the wall beside my bed and pressed it hard. The bed tilted and drapes parted with hardly a sound as I slid down the chute into the empty bath. The aquarium walls of the bathroom were a luminous green, and as I hastily made my way out, I could see the shadow of a ray swimming toward me. I turned the knob on the bathroom door. It wasn't locked, and I made my escape down the stairs. Indeed, my first thought was to go directly to Phoebe's room on the other side of the house. I certainly wanted to, but for all that I loved her, could I really trust her? She was, after all, a Jefferson; and I was, after all, just a guest, a guest who even now could not help but be awed by the pre-dawn magic of this house; by the cathedral walls covered with medieval tapestries; by the loitering stone and marble fauns, naiads, satyrs, soldiers, gorgons, gods, and goddesses, all pale as moonlight and bigger than life; by the carved ceilings so high above; by the emerald and turquoise rooms that each opened into other, even more magnificent rooms. Tall, jeweled lamps cast a roseate light, and pitch-velvet shadows concealed treasures that could only be imagined.

I rushed toward the atrium, where I thought I would escape into the gardens.

And I heard Phoebe screaming hysterically. "You'd better not have killed him. He'd *better* be alive."

I retraced my steps and waited behind an archway

near the ivory staircase. I wasn't surprised to see slaves pacing nervously on the landing above. Wordsworth and Isaac had obviously been sent to kill me, and perhaps Isaac had been given his chance to get back into the family's good graces.

But I *was* surprised to see Morgan step out of my room onto the landing; a very angry Phoebe was right behind him. I suppose Morgan had finally found his courage, although he seemed to have lost it again in Phoebe's presence.

"What the hell did you think you're doing, Morgan?" she shouted. Her voice seemed magnified by the dark, cavernous spaces. "He's my guest, you little twit, and what happens to him is *my* decision, not yours. Or Marion's."

"Marion has nothing to do with this," Morgan said. "It was all my idea. I just wanted to help you."

"Help me?"

"Anybody can see how much you're stuck on him, and you know Father isn't going to let you keep him, no matter what. He told me that before he left."

"Did not."

"He did too, and he practically told me to take care of things for him while he's gone because the more you fall in love with him, the more you're going to be hurt. And Marion thought that—"

"That's just what I thought," Phoebe said, but she did not continue because at just that moment everyone looked up into the grayness above, as though we could see through the ceiling. We could hear the sound of

aircraft overhead, and then there was a terrible concussion. I felt heat and was thrown backward. The ceiling shattered. The archway cracked and fell in a cloud of red dust and smoke before me.

More explosions.

Bombs falling, and I remembered my dream. Clumps of black soil falling. Black rain. Phoebe's tears. And, indeed, I was drenched. Water poured through cracks in what was left of the ceiling, which would soon give way; and the swimming sharks and rays and groupers and cuttlefish would fall onto the jewel-polished floor below.

Somehow, I had to rescue Phoebe, lest she be caught in the inevitable waterfall, a vertical tidal wave that would smash and splinter the balcony like balsa wood; but as I called out to her, my voice was swallowed by the staccato thunder-pumping of machine guns above. At least the slaves had the presence of mind to stand and fight. As I ran to the grand staircase, I met Marion and Morgan. We stopped for an instant, amid the cacophony of exploding bombs, machine guns, and the abdominal groaning of the castle. Water dripped like rain through the cracking and bulging ceiling high above. Morgan scowled at me, Marion called me a filthy something, and then I ran up the stairs to Phoebe while they, presumably, ran to the bunkers where they would be safe and sound and fitted out with champagne and caviar until the danger was over.

"Phoebe," I shouted, catching the back of her. She was running through the corridor, which curved

around the inside of the house like a mullah's ledge on a minaret. She heard me over the firing of machine guns and the thrumming shaking deafening exploding of bombs.

She stopped and shouted, "Mother," which I understood as code for "I've got to find Mother," and then disappeared into one of the many branching corridors. I followed her, my eyes and nose burning from smoke.

"You've got to—"

I meant "You've got to get off this floor now immediately run," but I seemed to run right through my words. I was intent on grabbing her up and getting out of the house, into the bunkers, perhaps, off this mountain; and then, in those heart-pounding exploding acrid smoke-smelling seconds I imagined that we'd somehow miraculously escaped from the mountain, from her father and family and everything associated with them, and I wondered whether she could live in the real world five minutes with me, without the insulation of millions—or billions—of dollars. It was idiocy even to dream of getting out, much less turning Phoebe into Suzy Housewife. In spite of the smoke and sudden heat, for the house was certainly on fire, although I couldn't see flames…yet, I think I grinned at the thought. But if I had the chance, the split-second chance of a lifetime, I'd take Phoebe away, without a dime in my pocket, I'd take her away for as long as she'd stand me.

But there *was* a chance. I was, after all, a prisoner. If the air strike was successful, as I imagined it would be,

then we would all be set free. The lads in the Pit would vouch for me. Perhaps there was a way to escape. To hide Phoebe, take enough diamonds and rubies to keep us more than comfortable in our new life.

Nonsense madness lunacy, yet those words had little meaning deep in this castle of impossibility where ceilings were layered with gold and walls of diamond and ruby glowed translucently like dreams in the deepest sleep; where hammerhead sharks could fall like rain, and God's machines could play music as well as orchestras.

I found Phoebe in her mother's suite, which was the size of most people's houses, and Phoebe turned to me and said, "She wouldn't've gone to the bunkers on her own, how could Morgan and Marion leave without her?" Phoebe was wild-eyed. "They hate her, that's why."

"Why wouldn't your mother go to the bunkers?" I asked, trying to bring her back to reason.

"She's claustrophobic. She can't stand darkness, can't stand to be without windows and light and—"

The sound of gunfire, the ceiling cracking, the house groaning, and then the expected waterfall, complete with all manner of fishes. Water poured over us, for the aquarium was two stories high, an aquatic crystalline house within the house, and I grabbed Phoebe and ran through the rain and wriggling, flapping, slapping fishes as the floors and walls and ceilings collapsed behind me, ran until I found another staircase, a narrow *escalier dérobé*. The smell of wet ash was thick as we

ran down the stairs, ran through the undecorated corridors used by servants, ran straight into blazing, blistering fire.

We found another way, which was blocked by the debris that had been ceiling and furniture, only moments ago. Coughing, panicking, we raced through darkness; now I was following Phoebe, who pulled me by the hand, down, down, into the damp stone cellars where we felt our way along the rough cold walls. Then an incline, the clanging of a heavy latch—Phoebe had found an exit. We pushed open a heavy door and looked up through the swirling smoke and soot to glimpse the dawn-pink sky.

The attack had been planned perfectly.

From an emplacement on the roof of an adjacent building…another burst of anti-aircraft guns. I could see only a few bodies of slaves scattered across the lawn; but in the dawn pinkness of this impossible morning, I couldn't see blood; nor could I smell the puke and feces of dying men, thank God, for the reek of gasoline, the acrid smoke, and the thunderstorm and metal odor of machine-guns firing on the roofs above were overpowering. I took a chance and stepped away from the castle to see what was in the sky; and you could've knocked me over with your pinky because the attackers-invaders-saviors, whatever they were, had just about everything in the air that could fly, all remainders from the war. Christ, there was a Vickers Gunbus, which hadn't been in service since 1916; and its gunner was strafing the slave quarters with his move-

able Lewis machine gun. There were several Jennys in the sky, and from the sound of it, I guessed they had been fitted out with 7.7 mm machine guns, just like the Gunbus. The Jenny was the favorite of most barnstormers, and I was no exception. While everything was happening around me—all the crashing and burning and exploding, I daydreamed about whisking Phoebe away in a Jenny, saving her from all this death and destruction; and I felt a sudden, unexpected rush of happiness. I would be saved, wouldn't have to spend my life a prisoner, or worse, become another one of those poisoned or strangled guests buried in an unmarked grave in the shallow soil of the diamond mountain. All that in a second, just like when I'd been in combat in the *Toulouse-the-Wreck*, the Spad that got me through Bloody April without so much as a bullet tearing through its delicate frame. I was again smelling oil and gasoline, hearing the peculiar and particular chinking sound of machine guns, and daydreaming. Time stretching, then collapsing, while my body, my hands and eyes, made all the moves.

Phoebe caught my arm, as though she had just read my mind and discovered my true thoughts of escaping with the enemy, and that's when I saw the twin-engined Handley Page 400, a British bomber that could carry a bomb load of around 1,800 pounds—Lord knows how they got their hands on *that*, and again, daydreaming, I wondered who they were. The bomber made a wide circle, and I asked Phoebe where the bunkers were because once that Handley Page started dropping her

guts, there wouldn't be much left to talk about.

"Look," Phoebe said, pointing, and, indeed, I saw slaves scrambling across the courtyard and leap-frogging up the inlaid tile perrons of the castle. They moved like trained and disciplined soldiers; the strafing fire of machine guns didn't deter them, even when two slaves were hit and fell backward over the stone steps.

We had to get out of here. I could hear the Handley Page's engines change tune as the great plane turned to begin its bombing run.

And then Phoebe shouted "Momma," and ran into the courtyard.

Sure enough, there was Giroma Jefferson strolling absently in her black chiffon evening dress embroidered with tiny beads.

I followed, but was too late: the Gunbus was strafing the courtyard, and in that second I felt time stretch out like some terrible gasoline-tainted gray wodge of taffy, wrapping itself around me...suffocating me. I saw Phoebe's mother fall, hit by the strafing fire, and Phoebe screaming and falling on top of her; and then it was like being in the cockpit of my Spad again, feeling once again absolutely focused yet numb, as I did during every dogfight. The numbness was fear, but it was a distant thing; and—as if I were a spectator still standing in the doorway of Jefferson's castle—I could see myself pulling Phoebe away from her mother and dragging her out of the courtyard. Phoebe screamed and tried to bite me before she came to her senses.

"I can't leave my mother," she said desperately. "She

might be alive, mightn't she?"

"No, darling," I said, "but don't think about that right now. We'll think about everything once you're safe. Now tell me where the bunkers are."

"There," and she pointed toward a strand of rocks where goats were trying to hide in the surrounding brush. "But we can't leave without Mother." So I picked up Mrs. Jefferson, who was just skin and bones, and we made our way under cover of the pine forest that was the west edge of Jefferson's zoo. I glimpsed zebras standing stock still, as if they were painted sculptures. Like Lot's wife, Phoebe looked back, seeking one last glimpse of paradise, and then we felt the concussion of an exploding bomb. For a few seconds, I could only hear a rushing, windy sound. I wasn't sure if the castle remained, as it was out of our sight from here; and we made our way, circuitously—keeping under cover—to the bunker. Phoebe pulled at an iron bar set cleverly into the rock—the camouflaged opening could only be detected if one already knew where it was—but nothing happened. I pulled the bar. Still nothing.

"They're in there, and they can hear us," Phoebe said to me. Turning to the cliff face of the bunker, she shouted, "Open the goddamn door, Morgan, you bastard. Mother's dead, and it's your fault."

But Morgan, if he was inside, was silent as the stone.

CHAPTER NINE

We laid Mrs. Jefferson out in the family mausoleum between the marble sepulchers of her father-in-law, the World's Greatest Liar, and his brother, who was murdered for the family cause. The cacophony of machine guns and bombs was reduced to great sighs and groans; only the dead held sway in this great marble shrine at the end of the gardens, and they ruled imperiously over the spiders and dust. Phoebe and I—and the cold and stiffening Mrs. Jefferson—were dwarfed by loggia of fifty-foot columns and pavilions that supported hordes of stone beasts and angels; and a huge equestrian statue of a Jefferson glowered down upon us like a marble god in his adamantine heaven. But there were no glowing onyx or pearl walls here, and not a diamond or a ruby or a sapphire in sight. This grand tomb might well have been designed by Phoebe's mother, who defied her wealth by never wearing a jewel. Perhaps she was the only one in the family who understood that you couldn't take it with you.

"I can't leave her here like this," Phoebe said, her eyes glistening with tears, and at that moment I felt I was more in love with her than ever before.

"It's not safe here."

"Pah! It's not safe anywhere," she said, suddenly gaining the weight and wisdom of the world.

"I'm getting you away from here this very minute," I said, and she turned to me, her face lit by anger and perhaps even hatred.

"That's my mother lying dead there, and you want to…you want to…"

"I want to get you to safety."

"You're as flat as my brother," she said, "and I'm not leaving."

"Then what *do* you propose to do?" I asked, trying to keep the frustration out of my voice. She turned away from me, leaned over her mother's corpse, and began to cry softly.

"It's all over."

She allowed me to put my arms around her and pull her away from her mother. "Poppa should have been here. He should have saved us. But he's too interested in…" She looked up at me and said, "*You* should have saved us. So what are we to do now, Mr. Orsatti?"

She turned back to her mother, as though she could somehow find all the answers behind those dead and closed eyes. She was shivering, trembling; and then, by sheer act of will, I should imagine, she straightened up and became absolutely calm. Her eyes narrowed in determination, and I saw her father in her heart-shaped perfect face. I saw in that instant the inevitability that she—and not her brother or sister or anyone else—would control everything. She was her father's

daughter; and love her as I did, I felt the sudden panicky urge to flee.

"I'm *not* giving everything up," Phoebe said firmly to her dead mother. "I won't, and they can't make me." Then she finally turned to me and said, "Well...?"

"Well, what?" I asked, and for that instant I felt like a nervous schoolboy. The muffled booming of bombs and the thick bursts of machine guns became louder. "We've got to get out of here right now!"

"Will you help me or not?" she asked, ignoring my last remark.

"Help you to do *what*?"

She stepped across the flawless marble floor and reached behind the stone sarcophagus of the World's Greatest Liar and strained as she pulled something. "Well, are you just going to stand there?"

She stepped back and allowed me to squeeze into the space behind the marble coffin. I felt the smooth metal bar she had been pulling at, which was ingeniously hidden under the curl of the coffin's lower rail, and released it without straining my back. The coffin slowly and smoothly slid down toward the wall, as if by magic, to reveal a dark catacomb fronted by dirty marble steps.

"Go on," Phoebe said; and when she saw my hesitation, she said, "Are you afraid I'd close you in?"

I must admit that a nervous thought had crossed my mind.

"Maybe I should, but I wouldn't," and she grinned at me, as if she'd forgotten everything for an instant; then

she took a last look at her mother, and led me down the steps and into the pit. She picked up a lantern from a ledge and scratched a match. Once the lantern radiated a halo of buttery light, she pulled at something in the wall. A rumbling echoed through what I imagined to be countless corridors, a hellish maze from which we would never escape; and I wanted to run back up the stone steps before the entrance was sealed. But the coffin fit into place like the last stone block of a pharaoh's tomb. The darkness seemed to sharpen my sense of smell. I breathed in the musty odors of the grave, and I was sure that this was a catacomb in the true sense—that bodies had been left to rot on shelves like the one where Phoebe had found her matches and lantern.

"Follow me," Phoebe said.

"What on Earth is this place?" I asked.

"You'll see."

"It's where your guests end up, isn't it?"

"Well, it's where *you* ended up."

"Answer me."

"I don't approve of overbearing men."

"Oh, I'm so very sorry," I said sarcastically. She hurried ahead, but I kept close to her. Our voices and movements echoed through the crudely cut corridor. "This place certainly wasn't cut out of diamond."

"Of course not, silly," Phoebe said. "The whole mountain isn't one big diamond."

"Your father said it was."

"Well, he's like my grandfather. He exaggerates.

About two-thirds of the mountain is one big diamond. The rest is this stuff, regular stone, I would suppose."

"And where does it lead?"

"Well, you're going to find out now, aren't you?" Phoebe said peevishly. Perhaps she was as frightened as I was, although I doubted that. She had obviously been here before. Probably many times. I shivered, swore, and slapped at something that had dropped onto my neck. Phoebe waved her lantern, which was smoking.

"Lots of spiders in this part. I hate them, don't you?" Phoebe said, quickening the pace.

I heard a screeing sound.

"And bats," she continued.

Which meant that there was another opening. But I was not relieved yet. We came to a terminus of sorts, and I heard water dripping and the distant rumbling of machinery. Phoebe led me through another corridor, which became narrower and narrower; her lantern threw cascading shadows across the rough-cut walls… and the reinforced metal doorway ahead.

Turning a large combination lock, which would unbolt the heavy door, she said, "We'll be fine now." The door was three feet thick; I'd only seen its kind in bank vaults. I helped her pull it open, and we were bathed in the dim but steady light that emanated from the opalescent walls and ceiling. I felt like I was back in the pit. There were no shadows in this place. We had entered a two-dimensional realm.

Phoebe led me through a long corridor that opened

into a large storeroom filled with rifles, machine guns, shotguns, pistols, flamethrowers, grenades and grenade launchers, all manner of knives and swords and bayonets, pull carts, sledge hammers, wire cutters, welding and carpenter's tools, cables, food-stuffs, canteens, medications, bandages, stretchers, gas masks, and canister weapons I didn't even recognize. "I think Poppa said this place is as secure as the bunker. Anyway, everything we need is right here."

"What are you looking for?" I asked warily, following her as she walked up one aisle and down another.

"You're the veteran of the Great War. You tell me." She walked on, then stopped and picked up what might have been a grenade. Behind her were shelves of gas masks and medicines: bleach ointments, clouded glass bottles of petrol, methylated spirits, kerosene, liquid paraffin, and carbon tetrachloride. There were swabs and eye drops and bandages and a metal mask with holes. I knew what *that* was for…what all that was for: mustard gas poisoning.

"No," I said, realizing that I had shouted. "No."

"We could gas them when they get out of their planes," Phoebe said excitedly, almost cheerfully. She walked a few paces down the aisle, stopped, and picked up what looked like an ordinary grenade launcher. Finding it unexpectedly heavy, she nearly dropped it. "Here, we can use these tubes to shoot them off with. I think these go with the gas grenades. Poppa showed me once, but I'm not so sure now."

"I won't have any part of cold-blooded murder."

Phoebe raised her eyebrow slightly, as if mystified. "I don't want to *kill* them, just put them to sleep for a while." Then her face reddened and she said, "What do you think they did to Mother...and our servants? Well...?"

I nodded—there was nothing I could say to that—and examined the canister she had been holding, and the others neatly laid out on the gunmetal shelves like condiments for a deadly banquet. "Well, you'll certainly put them to sleep for a good long while with this. It's phosgene, for Chrissakes. The Germans used it at Ypres in 1915." I *thought* I could smell a faint odor of new mown hay, which is a dead giveaway for phosgene. "If I can smell it, something must be leaking. Let's get *out* of here now."

"I like the smell, don't you?" Phoebe said, teasing me.

"Phoebe!"

"Phoebe what, you flat tire. How could you believe for even one second that I would actually consider killing those men?" She seemed to be about to break into tears. "Well, I don't need your help, after all. I can do it myself."

"What? Kill all those aviators? And how do you propose to do that all alone? You could get a few of them, I'll admit, but not all of them."

"I told you I'm not going to kill *any* of them," Phoebe said, and she looked so angry that I thought she might actually stamp her foot. Or throw the canister at me. "Come over here."

"We need to get out of here," I said. "We've probably already poisoned ourselves."

"Well, I've been down here only about two hundred times, and it always smells like this, and I'm still alive, so stop being a stupid coward."

I felt my ears burn.

She walked over to me and asked in almost a whisper, "Are you going to trust me?"

After a time I said, "Yes," and put my arms around her.

"Then you'll help me?"

"Of course I will." I felt the last tuggings of my conscience and wondered if, indeed, I would be killing those aviators.... For those few seconds as I held Phoebe close, I could hear her shallow breathing and the ever so faint booming of bombs.

And somehow I *knew* I was making a great mistake...

Then she kissed me, tenderly but without passion, and said, "Let's get ready. If you can pile up the little gas bombs and the tubes, I'll try to get us some more help."

"What do you mean?"

"I mean that I know the way to the servants' quarters," Phoebe said, "and I'll bet you dollars to doughnuts that some of the servants are using the tunnels like bunkers. If they're there, I'll find them."

"I should be with you."

"No, we've got to make sure the enemy doesn't land before we can get out there. If you just keep following the tunnels to your right, you'll come to the outside.

Don't worry, I'll find you somewhere between here and there." Phoebe nodded toward a corridor that curved to the right. The light made the far wall and the branching corridors look flat, as though the tunnels, as Phoebe called them, had been lightly sketched with a charcoal pencil. Phoebe turned and looked back toward where we had come. She seemed to be staring at something only she could see, and her eyes were bright with tears.

"Phoebe..."

"They killed her," she said, meaning her mother, and then she disappeared into the flat light. I called after her, and her voice echoed back, "Make sure you take the right bombs."

And I wondered once again if the *right* bombs would be lethal.

I followed Phoebe's directions, kept turning to the right, and navigated the warren of corridors until I reached a camouflaged opening in the hill west of the chateau. Phoebe and I had spent many a perfect hour watching the zebras play and frolic through these gently inclined fields, and the sweet fragrances of spring flowers and Phoebe's perfume were cold memories as I looked out at the devastation before me. It was a clear morning with just a touch of chill...and the smells of oil and metal. Through the copses of evergreens and oak, I could see the blackened chateau and the ruined grounds of what the Old Man had called his enchanted hill. A streamer of smoke rose from the castle's west wing, yet, miraculously, most of the castle was untouched. A bomb had obliterated the Neptune

pool and the great Grecian marble steps.

Above, in the blue, ceramic sky, planes circled like buzzing insects waiting their turn to land.

We were probably too late. At least half the planes would already be on the ground and the aviators, probably armed to the teeth, would be making their way to the chateau. I had enough gas canisters in the pull cart to asphyxiate half the population of Chicago. I waited for Phoebe and had begun to worry when I heard footsteps. Phoebe had indeed found a squad of servants, including Robert, who, surely, was too old and decrepit for this kind of operation. Yet he stood in front of the other slaves.

"We're ready," Phoebe said, looking at me determinedly, as if waiting for me to respond with the proper etiquette. She stood away from me, waiting, testing me, and I knew if I didn't respond properly, I would lose her forever.

I nodded to Robert and asked him if he knew how to launch the gas grenades.

"Yes, Mr. Orsatti, I certainly do, and so do my men."

"Your men?" I asked, glancing at Phoebe, who did not seem disturbed, just anxious to get underway.

"Yes, I trained them. Under Mr. Jefferson's orders, of course."

"And who trained you?" I asked.

"I believe he was an ordnance sergeant, whom Mr. Jefferson invited for a visit. Miss Phoebe took quite a shine to him, if I remember correctly." There was an underlying meanness in his soft, pliant voice; and it

was obvious that he viewed my condescension as intolerable. "Isn't that so, Miss Phoebe?"

Ignoring him, Phoebe asked me if I was ready.

I nodded and picked up a grenade. Robert did the same, and attached it to the launcher; indeed, he knew what he was doing. He then picked up a gas mask from the pull cart and pulled it over his face to be at the ready. The others followed in turn. Before Phoebe could pull her gas mask over her face, I said, "Phoebe, why don't you stay…."

"Don't even suggest it," she said.

* * * * * * *

Moving quickly, we made our way under cover toward the landing strip north of the chateau. I deployed the men along the way with orders to fire if they saw the enemy, even if there were other slaves nearby who might inhale the gas—after all, the grenades *should* not kill.

However, there was no time to wait and ponder.

By the time we reached the rocky outcrops near the landing strip, we were in the thick of it. Half a dozen pilots were already making their way toward the chateau, and they were armed and at the ready. They saw us at the same time we saw them, and we both took cover. They began firing, and Isaac calmly launched a grenade at them, which exploded with a low thumping sound. I watched through smeary goggles and heard my breath wheezing through the mask, which smelled of rubber and formaldehyde. After a few moments, the

aviators stopped firing. We waited and then moved forward cautiously. I feared the worst, but when we examined them, they were indeed still breathing; one pilot was snoring, as if happily tucked into his bed. We wasted no time pulling the sleepers under cover so they could not be seen. Then we moved forward to keep an eye on the planes as they landed. They kept a tight formation. Impressive. As each plane taxied down the turf of the golf-course runway, the pilots who had just landed stayed close to provide possible covering fire. We waited behind copses of weeping willows. It was too easy to gas the aviators, take their weapons, and drag them under cover—we were shooting the proverbial ducks in a barrel—and like everything that seems too easy, there was a snag. We miscalculated.

One of the aviators had somehow managed to get past us and circle around to our rear. He was wearing one of our gas masks, which he must have taken from one of the servants on the way; and he shot three of our servants with his automatic rifle before we could retaliate. To my surprise, Phoebe shot him squarely through the forehead with a handgun.

Robert sprayed the area with machine-gun fire and ordered his squad of servants to move forward.

More gunfire and the chuff chuffing of canister.

Then silence, a heavy awkward silence, as though some sort of geologic time or consensual dream had been replaced by a darker, more sinister reality.

As we moved forward, I could see faint wisps of gas roiling in the fetid air. Above me was a clear blue sky,

as innocent as day. I looked around for Phoebe, but she had suddenly disappeared. "Robert, where's Phoebe?" I asked, and then I heard a series of shots from the trees behind us. Each shot seemed to be timed.

Robert just looked at me.

Of course, he knew...

And a moment later, so did I.

* * * * * * *

I found Phoebe beyond the landing strip near the cover of trees and brush. Facemask and goggles hid most of her perfect face...it was as if someone else was committing the terrible deed.

"Stop!" I shouted, my voice muffled by my own gas mask.

Phoebe looked up at me blankly, raised her rifle reflexively toward my chest...and I felt strong arms lift me into the air as my own rifle clattered to the ground.

Isaac—the slave who had been my "bodyguard"—didn't relax his hold on me, even while Phoebe calmly continued to execute the sleeping pilots.

CHAPTER TEN

"I can't believe that she has received any of my messages," I said.

Robert lowered his great wrinkled head and said, "All you have sent has been received by Miss Jefferson." He stood before my makeshift bed in the guest library where I'd been imprisoned...upon Miss Jefferson's orders.

Isaac stood by the door, his bulk taking up most of the doorway.

The north wing had survived intact, and I wondered why I was being kept here. Perhaps the other rooms, the bedrooms, had secret exits. Or perhaps Robert was right and Phoebe thought I'd keep myself occupied with her father's books and the Steinway grand piano that sat like a great white gold-crested bird in the center of the library. I'd practiced most of the days and nights; the suppleness had returned to my fingers, and I indulged myself with Berg's atonalities and the cloying wretchedness of Mahler's *lieder*. Jefferson's collection of leather-bound volumes and first editions were, indeed, glorious, and it had taken me two weeks to replace the books back on the shelves in alphabetical

order. It was as if an earthquake had struck the chateau, or what remained of it.

"Will there be anything else you wish this morning, Mr. Orsatti?" Robert asked. "A bath, perhaps...? I've laid out your clothes, just in case." He bowed and smiled condescendingly.

"Just in case of what?" I asked.

"Why, in case you might wish to change, sir."

I waved him away. The door clicked shut, the key turned in the lock, and I was alone. I had not shaved, nor bathed. My hair needed trimming, my pajamas smelled as sour as my breath, and I was wallowing in self-pity. I didn't feel like reading, studying, or even playing, which was most unusual. Instead I mused on the possibilities of escape. I had tried everything I could think of, from picking the door lock (impossible!), to working the bars loose on the high windows, to holding Robert hostage—but somehow the old servant had managed to break two of my ribs before Isaac overpowered me—and all I had accomplished trying to get past the bars was to break the window glass.

So Robert had won, and I had lost.

We both knew that he was not my servant. But I was certainly his prisoner.

To add insult to injury, it was yet another magnificent morning. Golden sunlight poured in from the gardens, and the grounds were alive with hammering and shouting and the grinding and creaking and groaning of heavy machinery. The chateau was being

repaired…rebuilt, and I had been imprisoned in this room for almost two months.

At least when I was in the Pit I had had company...

I padded back and forth barefoot on the Persian carpets. I examined Jefferson's astonishing collection of Greek vases that were secured to the hand-carved bookcases in case there might be an earthquake. Well, there *was* an earthquake, and it originated in the skies! I plonked my fingers over the keys as I passed the piano. I took a bit of toast and bacon from the silver tray Isaac had laid on an overly ornate gilt bronze table designed by Pelagio Palagi. I picked up my rose porcelain coffee cup and paced.

I had ruined everything…

No, *Phoebe* had ruined everything.

I wolfed down breakfast and swore once again that if Phoebe ever had the gall to come anywhere near me, I would—

There was a light tapping on the door.

I knew who it was. I *knew*...

"Go away."

A key turned in the lock, the doorknob turned, and the door groaned open. Phoebe stood in the doorway, looking small, uncertain, and breathtakingly lovely. She wore a simple pleated blue skirt with a white pullover. Her blond hair was pulled back, rolled, and tied with a golden ribbon that was the same color as the gilded trefoil arches over my prison bar windows. She stepped into the room, leaving the door ajar. Her face colored as she looked at me. She lowered her eyes,

then, as if catching herself, looked directly at me.

"Where are your bodyguards?" I asked, more harshly than I'd anticipated. "Surely they're waiting in the hall in case I try something funny."

"What could you try that would be funny?" she asked in a low voice, and for only an instant, there was merriment in her eyes, which were bright, as though she'd been crying.

"What do you want?"

"What do you think…?"

"Don't answer my question with a question. You at least owe me an explanation. I've been in here for… months."

"I don't owe anybody an explanation, and you've only been here for five weeks and a day," she said, then looked down at the carpet again. "I'm sorry, Paul. I'm getting this all wrong…"

"What are you talking about?" I asked, sitting down on the end of the long gold brocade couch. My eggs were glassy-looking in the plate on the table before me. My coffee was cold, but I drank it anyway; I felt awkward, as I always did around her, and I needed something to do with my hands. After the coffee, I lit a cigarette, and Phoebe asked if she could have one, too. She bent over me while I lit her cigarette, and I could smell her perfume, see the light in her hair, and I caught my breath.

"Please don't be angry with me," she said, standing behind the table, as though afraid to sit down beside me. I gestured her to do so, but she stood her ground,

closed her eyes for a beat, then said, as if reciting, "I had no choice but… No, that's no good. None of it's any good." Then she sat down and against all my better judgment, I was caught by her…again. But she didn't seem to know. Her eyes filled with tears and she said, "How you must hate me."

I moved toward her, then caught myself. "I don't hate you."

"Yes, you do. I remember how you looked at me. I'll never forget the horror and disgust on your face. I—"

I didn't say anything.

"But I have to live with what I've done. Somehow…"

I could only nod.

"I've tried to come up with a way to tell you, to explain. Every day I prepared a speech, but I…I just couldn't."

"So you just left me here to rot."

"I told Robert to look after you."

"You know what *that* means," I said.

She nodded, and I saw that she had used too much rouge on her cheeks to give her color; her perfect, dimpled face looked strained, and I detected worry lines on the corners of her pale blue eyes. "I know…I was selfish, but I couldn't think. I didn't want to lose you, so I—"

"Yes, Phoebe, we know what you did. Now what do you want to tell me?" Those words sounded cruel, even to my ears, and I regretted them immediately. Foolishly, stupidly, impossibly, I didn't want to lose her. It didn't matter what she had done.

Too late. She stood up, as if I had slapped her. "Yes, of course, you're right."

"What do you want to tell me?" I asked quickly, and I found myself standing also.

"I want to tell you that...I don't know. I can't do it now. It was a terrible mistake—" and she turned to run out the door.

I caught her, held her close, and although her breath was ragged, she didn't cry. She stiffened, then rested her face against mine and said, "All right, I can tell you now. I don't regret killing those men. I didn't then. I don't now. I know I was wrong, I know I'll burn in hell forever, God forgive me, but they *murdered* Momma. I couldn't help it. It was like someone else was killing them, even while I was doing it. Maybe it was because I found out about Father, maybe—"

"What about your father?" I asked.

She pulled away from me and sat back down on the couch. She took a puff on her cigarette, which was still burning in the ashtray, as was mine. The smoke roiled in the sunlight like clouds, or gas. "I'll tell you everything, but I need to know..."

"What...?"

"I know you can't forgive me, but will you listen?"

"Yes, I just told you that."

"I'll tell you everything," Phoebe repeated, "but..."

"But what?" I asked.

She shook her head, and tears stained her makeup. Then she straightened up, composed herself, and said, "I kept you here because I love you. Selfishly. I knew

you'd try to escape. I was even going to give you a choice. I was going to ask you whether you'd rather go back down to the Pit to be with your friends." She laughed, puffed her cigarette, and smashed it out in the ashtray.

"But you weren't going to let me be your confidant and stay with you."

"I…I needed time to—"

Instead of listening, I went on, caught up in my own anger. "And you certainly weren't going to let me leave the mountain."

"No," she said. "I'm crazy about you, but I'm not stupid. God help me, I'm my father's daughter." Before I could say anything, she continued. "I had to work things out. I told you…I needed time."

"You could have come to me anytime," I said.

She nodded. "I've tried…every single day. I guess I can now. Now that Father is back."

I felt a chill tickle down my spine. It was over. All over. If Jefferson was back in charge, he'd figure a way to dispose of me sooner rather than later…once he got around Phoebe. Or perhaps he wouldn't even have to do that.

"No, Paul, you don't understand," Phoebe said. "Will you come with me? And then you can decide."

"Decide what?" I asked. "Whether to stay up here or go back to the Pit?"

But Phoebe was waiting for me at the door…as were Robert and Isaac.

* * * * * * *

I must have been favoring my right side a bit as we walked because Phoebe asked me what was the matter. I glanced at Robert, then asked, "Didn't he tell you?"

"Tell me what?" Phoebe asked.

"Ask *him*."

"Well, Robert…?"

He started talking to her in dialect, but I interrupted. "In English, Robert."

So Robert explained that he had broken my ribs—by mistake—and Phoebe dismissed him then and there. Isaac, however, was retained, presumably to guard me from Phoebe. I couldn't help gloating, and defended Robert as my servant.

"You see, you're learning," Phoebe said to me as we climbed the servants' staircase to the third floor. She unlocked the door to old man Jefferson's bedroom and study, which was surprisingly modest…except for the wildly ornate Spanish ceiling crafted from gilded wood and an eighteenth-century bed with a satin canopy and matching bedspread. There was a simple desk and cushioned chair beside the bed, a small fireplace that needed cleaning, and family portraits on the walls. The desk was piled with papers and an odd mechanism that seemed to sit on the desk but was supported by what looked like a drainpipe that disappeared into the floor. There were folders on the floor around the desk and the pipe, along with women's underclothing and various scattered skirts and dresses. Obviously Phoebe's. "I've taken Poppa's room," she continued. "It's a bit messy, but that's because I won't allow the servants in here."

With that she pushed the door closed on Isaac. "You see, now I'm alone with you and at your mercy."

I nodded and she apologized.

"No need," I said, but she had already forgotten and was rummaging for something in the covers of her bed.

"Here they are," she said, finding what she was looking for: a large envelope containing photographs of her father and a dark-haired, finely featured girl. "You see, she's younger than me. Can you beat that? It's the bunk. The fucking bunk."

I was surprised, as I'd never heard Phoebe swear before, but she just glared at those photographs and blinked back tears.

"Who is she?" I asked.

"Poppa's whore, that's who she is. Mother's dead because of her. Poppa promised that he'd make her a film star. Here, look for yourself," and she took a handful of letters from the desk and practically threw them at me.

"Easy," I said. "I'm not the enemy."

"Maybe you are…maybe you aren't. We'll see, won't we?"

As I glanced at the embarrassingly fraught yet boastful love letters, Phoebe continued. "Her name is Greta Gustafsson, but Poppa changed her name to Garbo because he thought Gustafsson sounded like it could be a Jew name, although anybody would know it was Scandinavian. And he hired his pervert friend Mauritz Stiller to pimp for her. Do you know who he is?"

I confessed I didn't.

"He made that sex film *Erotikon* back in 1920."

I shrugged.

"Poppa showed it to me in the theater. He laughed all the way through it. It wasn't that bad, I suppose, but it was trash. Like her." Phoebe took the photographs from me. "Well, her career is down the drain. I've seen to *that*."

"What have you done?"

"Taken Poppa back, the filthy snake in the grass double-crossing, double-dealing—"

"Phoebe..."

She hunched over the bed and wept. "He murdered Mother and sold us out. The dirty bastard." Then she shook her head, tried to smile at me, and said, "I found it all out from Uncle George."

"Uncle George?" I asked. "He's crazy...and he's in the Pit."

"He knows more than you think. He's got ways of knowing everything, and the slaves trust him. It was Robert who passed on his messages, and because of you, I've probably lost a good slave forever."

"Because of *me*?"

"Well, slave or not, he shouldn't've broken your ribs and treated you like a bump."

"Phoebe, about your father?"

"He sold us all out. He brought in the planes and the bombs and the gunfire. After he changed his name and converted most of the money."

"I can't believe he'd do all that, just for a little bit of

cheesecake."

"It was getting too dangerous to keep the mountain," Phoebe said. "Uncle George explained it all to me. It was so simple. Father allowed that pilot to get away from us, or could have allowed it, anyway. Once the mountain was found out, then the market for diamonds would crash, which is why Poppa started putting his money into...radium. Now he thought that would be perfectly safe, but he was wrong about that, too." She paused and stared at the contraption on the desk. "Poppa thought of most everything, I've got to hand him that. He'd even made sure that two of the aviators who tried to invade us were reporters, just to make certain that the word got out properly."

"It doesn't make sense that he would give up everything," I said.

"Did you read those letters?"

"Still..."

"And he wasn't giving up hardly anything. Only us. He'd end up with more money than he had, once the government clamped down on the diamond market, which Uncle George says would certainly happen. Poppa has hidden diamonds everywhere you could imagine."

"I can't imagine he'd harm his family. And family tradition was so important to him."

She chuckled. "So was his freedom, and he figured that we'd be let off. He probably also figured we'd all be safe in the bunkers. But he knew Mother wouldn't go to the bunker because of her claustrophobia. He

knew that, and he killed her just as sure as if he pulled the trigger."

"But he came back," I said.

"Yes, Paul. I *brought* him back."

"How?"

"Uncle George. He knows everything Poppa knows. He and I...became Poppa, and used the slaves and his contacts to chase him down. We caught him buck naked with his mistress. I've got more photographs, but Uncle George is against letting the press have them."

"I should imagine he would be."

"And so am I...of course."

I nodded and watched her walk over to the desk and adjust the contraption.

"Come here, Paul, and I'll show you how Poppa kept an eye on everything."

I followed her to the desk, and she turned a switch that engaged gears below us—I could hear them shift. She directed me to look into the concave glass that covered the large pipe. For an instant everything looked ghostly and smeary, as if I were gazing at a crystal ball, and then my eyes grew accustomed to the images. I was looking into a room lit by uniform light. Looking down. Looking at Randolph Estes Jefferson, the old man himself. God.

"Can you see him?" Phoebe asked.

I nodded, fascinated. The room looked slightly askew, curved somehow, as if the edges were being pulled upward.

"It's hard to see sometimes."

"What's he *doing*?" I asked. He seemed to be kneeling beside his bed, except the bed was transparent as a diamond.

"That's the biggest diamond in the world…except for the mountain, of course," Phoebe said.

"Is he praying to it?"

Phoebe laughed mirthlessly. "He asked to have it sent down. It was all he wanted."

"Why?" I asked.

"Because it's perfect," Phoebe said. "Poppa has had I don't know how many diamond cutters working on it. They're all in the tunnels."

"You mean they're dead," I said.

She nodded.

I gazed at the stone, which seemed to be suffused with blue light.

"He calls it God's Blue, and I don't know what he's doing with it now. I eavesdropped on him when I first sent it down. He tried making some sort of deal with God. If God would turn everything around like it was before he left, he would give up all his sins and build God a diamond cathedral. Silly, but I guess he's quite mad." She looked at me—I could feel her staring at me—and said, "But no more mad than the rest of us, I suppose."

"Are you just going to leave him there?" I asked.

"Until he drops dead," Phoebe said quietly.

"Have you talked to him?"

"I'll never speak to him again, but Uncle George visits him regularly and makes sure he eats."

"The other men will kill him."

"No, they can't get to him. Poppa is perfectly safe." After a pause, Phoebe asked if I wanted to say hello to Uncle George. She turned one switch on and another off and said, "Hello, Uncle George."

I could see Uncle George looking straight up at us. He had been fiddling with his trains, which were all speeding around the miniature countryside with great electrical abandon.

"Hello, Phoebe."

"He can't see us," Phoebe said.

"Phoebe…are you there?" George asked.

"Yes, I'm here, and so is Paul Orsatti."

"Aha, so you've finally gotten up the courage to pop the question."

"Not yet, Uncle George," Phoebe said.

"Ah…? So why then are you calling me?"

"To ask you to come up and help us."

"You're doing just fine, Phoebe," George said. "You don't need me up there. You've got Paul… Hi, Paul."

"Hi, George," I said.

"No, I had more than enough of 'up there' when I was up there. Now stop watching me walk around in my underwear and fix things up with Paul. Bye, Paul."

"Bye, George," I said.

Phoebe clicked off the contraption.

"Well?" I asked. "What did George mean about popping the question?"

"What do you think he meant?"

"Stop it, Phoebe, and answer me."

"It's just what you probably think." She looked intently at the carpet and whispered, "Do you want to marry me?"

I was going to say yes immediately, but something caught in my throat. I wanted to rush to her, envelop her in my arms, and protect her. She was the pearl beyond price, the object of my desire. She looked perfect standing before me, her ribbon golden in the sunlight streaming through arched windows, her face flawless; and yet suddenly she seemed…flat, featureless like the denizens of dreams, dangerous creatures that suddenly appear, that *look* familiar, but are something else entirely.

Phoebe looked pale and white and fragile. She looked up at me and said, "You see…? There, I have your answer."

"I haven't said *anything* yet."

"Which says it all, doesn't it."

"No," I said. "I love you."

"But…"

"No buts."

"Then you'll marry me…?"

I nodded and started to move toward her, but she took a step backward.

"And you'd be willing to live here?" she asked.

"You mean as a prisoner?"

"No, as my husband."

"Would I be a prisoner?"

"You would be my husband," she said; and I felt a thrill of possibility…that I would be with her, but more

than that…that I could change things, I could—

"And as my husband, you would respect the way things are," Phoebe said.

"What do you mean by that?"

"The way we live…the way we are."

"Of course, but we can make things better."

She looked away from me, as if considering. Then she said, "We *will* make things better. It's already happening. I'm rebuilding everything Poppa and those pilots destroyed. I hate pilots—except for you, darling." She smiled at me, as though I had provided her with all the answers. "We could make everything ever so much better. Poppa didn't think smart enough. We'll camouflage everything, so even if planes fly overhead, they won't see anything but rocks. Of course, it won't be rocks." She hugged me and said, "You're brilliant. I'll tell Uncle George about your idea, and he'll figure out how to do it. He won't want to stay down there in the Pit anymore. He *loves* to solve problems…."

Phoebe must have seen something register on my face because she stopped talking and gave me a quizzical look. "But that wasn't what you meant, was it? So who *do* you want to make things better for?" she demanded. "The servants? The prisoners in the Pit?"

"Both, for a start."

I understood then that this mountain was the only thing that was real for Phoebe. She would never leave it for very long…or change it.

Her eyes suddenly became moist. "Poppa told me you'd be as selfish and greedy as all the rest of them."

She turned away from me and walked out the door.
    And I realized that I still loved her more than ever.

CHAPTER ELEVEN

I shouted "Pung" and concentrated on our game of mah-jongg while Uncle George's Lionel trains steamed and clattered around us. George was a good player… and he'd assured me that Phoebe would probably take me back once I saw the light of reason.

It was simply a matter of time…and conscience.

ABOUT THE AUTHOR

JACK DANN is a multiple-award winning author who has written or edited over seventy-five books, including the ground-breaking novels *The Man Who Melted*, *The Memory Cathedral*—which is an international bestseller, the Civil War novel *The Silent*, which *Library Journal* called "narrative storytelling at its best...most emphatically recommended," and *Bad Medicine*, which has been compared to the works of Jack Kerouac and Hunter S. Thompson. His counterfactual biography *The Rebel: an Imagined Life of James Dean* has been called "a love letter to the 60's" and "a significant and very gripping novel." A companion James Dean short story collection entitled *Promised Land* has also been published in Great Britain, as has Dann's most recent short novel *The Economy of Light*. His short fiction can be found in collections such as *Timetipping, Jubilee, Visitations*, and *The Fiction Factory*. His latest anthologies are *Dreaming Again, The Dragon Book* (with Gardner Dozois), and *Australian Legends* (with Jonathan Strahan).

Dann is a recipient of the Nebula Award, the Australian Aurealis Award (twice), the Ditmar Award

(four times), the World Fantasy Award, the Peter McNamara Achievement Award, the Peter McNamara Convenors Award for Excellence, and the Premios Gilgamés de Narrativa Fantástica award. He has also been honored by the Mark Twain Society (Esteemed Knight). Dann lives in Australia on a farm overlooking the sea and "commutes" back and forth to Los Angeles and New York. He is married to the writer Janeen Webb. His website is

www.jackdann.com